MW01146135

BE STILL MY HEART

A DEAR ABBY COZY MYSTERY - BOOK 2

SONIA PARIN

"Be Still My Heart" Copyright © 2018 Sonia Parin
All Rights Reserved

No part of this publication may be reproduced in any form or by any
means, without the prior written permission of the author, except in the
case of brief quotations embodied in critical articles and reviews.

This is a work of fiction. Names, characters, places and incidents are the
product of the author's imagination or are used fictitiously. Any
resemblance to actual persons, living or dead, organisations, events or
locales is entirely coincidental.

vFeb20

ISBN: 9781720136309

CHAPTER 1

"*A*re you mad? If you print this, the whole town will rise up against you and then I'll have to write your obituary. Abby Maguire, who would have guessed you'd turn out to be such a killjoy?"

Abby waved at a passer-by and then looked at Faith. The young Eden Rise Gazette office assistant sat at her desk scowling.

"You haven't listened to a word I've said," Faith complained.

Abby swung her feet off the desk and sat up. "I have been listening and every word in that article I wrote is true. The world is running out of cocoa beans putting the production of chocolate at risk. I'm merely reporting a scientific fact."

Faith gave a slow shake of her head. Tapping her computer screen, she said, "This is irresponsible reporting. I'm afraid I'll have to put my foot down. I know

I'm only the office assistant here, but I have a say in what is included in the weekly paper."

"Faith, you play a pivotal role in the Eden Rise Gazette and I wouldn't be able to do my job without your valuable assistance, but the story will go ahead." Abby tried to keep a straight face. "People need to know."

Faith looked around the office. When her gaze landed on the storefront window, she grimaced. "People will throw stones through the window. I can picture the mob, armed with pitchforks and crying for your blood."

"Nonsense. You underestimate the average person's desire to be kept informed."

Faith pursed her lips. "The writing is atrocious."

"What?" Abby leaned forward and looked at her computer screen. "The delicate cacao plant is under threat as rising temperatures are sucking moisture from the soils where the trees grow." She looked up. "What's wrong with that?"

"It's morbid." Faith threw her hands up in the air. "Experts believe the cacao plant will be impossible to grow after the year 2050. That's within my lifetime. How could you?"

Abby could barely contain her laughter. "I'm sure we'll all find a substitute for chocolate. Did you know there's a fruit that tastes like chocolate?" Abby did a quick search online. "*The Black Sapote*, otherwise known as the chocolate pudding fruit. It grows in Florida, the Philippines and there's an Australian variety called *Bernicker*. See, all's well. In fact, it's even better than that because you get to eat healthy chocolate."

"Are you quite finished?"

"You feel really strongly about this." Abby cocked her head in amusement. "I read the article to Doyle last night and he seemed to like it."

"Doyle? He's a dog and he doesn't eat chocolate. What would he know?" Faith wagged her finger at Abby. "The ink on your contract with Sebastian Cavendish is not dry yet. I'm sure there's a cooling off period and once he hears of this—"

Abby laughed. "You think this is grounds for dismissal?" Sebastian Cavendish owned one of the largest newspapers in the country as well as a few international ones. Abby would be lucky if he spent two minutes thinking about the Eden Rise Gazette, a small town weekly newspaper he had inherited from his grandfather. They were lucky he'd chosen to keep it running…

"Fine. Run the article, but don't blame me when you're chased out of town. We've taken you in, we've accepted you and treated you as one of our own and this is the thanks we get. You're asking for trouble, Abby Maguire." Faith continued muttering under her breath as she got busy working on the layout for the next edition of the Eden Rise Gazette.

"Coffee?" Abby offered. "I'm headed down to Joyce's Café."

"Throw in some cake and I might decide to forgive you. Oh, and hurry back. We still need to put the finishing touches to the annual picnic announcement. The posters are going up tomorrow but I think it'll be a great idea if we run it first."

The timing could not have been better, Abby thought. The town was still recovering from the recent loss of one of its most prominent members. The owner of the Gazette, Dermot Cavendish, had been greatly admired by everyone. Instead of fading, his memory was kept alive. Not a day went by when she didn't hear his name weaving into a conversation.

Grabbing Doyle's harness she strode out of the newspaper office only to stop and say, "I suppose this isn't the best time to let you know I'll be doing a follow up article about the possible extinction of bees. That means no more honey…"

Growling, Faith muttered something about fire and brimstone raining upon her.

Abby drew out her cell phone and checked the time. "In ten, nine, eight…" The town clock struck the hour and her cell phone rang. "Hi, mom."

"I can't see you."

Ever since Abby had landed in the small town of Eden, 8,000 plus miles away from her previous home in Seattle, her mom had insisted they video chat at least once a week. If it were up to her, they'd be connected 24/7. Then again, her mom lived in Iowa, the safest state in which to live and she couldn't help worrying about

Abby who'd uprooted her life to trek half way around the world for a job. Strangely, her mom had never worried when Abby had lived and worked in Seattle.

Abby bobbed her head from side to side as she thought Seattle didn't have the world's deadliest critters crawling around the place. Although, she had yet to encounter any of them here…

Adjusting the angle of her cell phone, she asked, "Can you see me now?"

"Yes, now show me the rest."

Abby sighed. Her mom needed to know Dermot Cavendish's death had been an isolated incident.

"It's just a regular day here in Eden, mom. We had some morning frost but the sun is out now. People are looking forward to the annual picnic by the lake. I'll be headed there later on to take some photos." She turned the corner into the main street and saw Joyce Breeland outside her café holding a straw hat and…

"What? What's happened?" her mom asked. "Your eyebrows just shot up."

"Oh… well. Remember Joyce?"

"Yes, of course I do. She's lovely and I simply adore how she dresses. You should get some tips from her."

A walking fashion statement. Joyce Breeland loved her costumes. "She's…" Abby searched for the right word. "Thrusting a hat at someone." As she came closer, Abby recognized the man with Joyce. Bradford Mills, Joyce's fiancé and the owner of the local antique store, Brilliant Baubles. "What's the name of those hats worn in the 1920's?" Abby clicked her fingers. "They're boating hats. I'm sure they're also worn by students at Oxford and Cambridge."

"A Spencer boating hat," her mom said.

"That's it." Why would Joyce use one as a weapon?

"What's happening now? Show me," her mom demanded.

Joyce just hit Bradford with the hat...

Abby ran the words through her mind and tried to imagine her mom's reaction. It wouldn't be good. "I think Joyce is trying to make a point. I'm too far away to show you."

"Well, walk faster."

Abby looked down at Doyle and nudged her head. "Come on, Doyle. The suspense will make my mom jittery." When she got within earshot of the couple, Abby sighed. "Mom, I think they're just having a friendly discussion about proper boating attire." And Bradford Mills appeared to be dead set against wearing a ridiculous straw hat.

"Are you attending this picnic?" her mom asked.

"Yes, of course," Abby confirmed. "I have to write about it."

"And what are you going to wear?" her mom asked.

Abby hadn't given it any thought.

"Are you going with someone?"

She really hadn't given it any thought.

"What about that lovely detective? You could ask him. After all, this is a charity event. He should be prepared to do his bit."

Abby didn't want to read too much into her mom's

suggestion. Although… Did she actually see her as a charity case? "Joshua is busy."

"What with? Has someone else been murdered?"

"No, of course not. He's busy with other police duties. You know… maintaining law and order."

"But he's a detective. They only deal with serious crimes."

Abby didn't want to mention the recent case of arson or the sudden rise in car thefts in the next town.

Seeing her, Joyce beckoned her over. "Abby, just the person to weigh in on this."

Abby smiled at Bradford who gave her a small nod of acknowledgment and said, "I bet anything Abby is not going to dress up for the picnic. Hello, Mrs. Maguire."

"Please, call me Eleanor," her mom said, "I hear you're all going on a picnic."

"Yes," Joyce chirped. "And I have the perfect outfit for it. It's a pleated skirt with a sailor sweater, all in eggshell white. Bradford is wearing eggshell white trousers with a matching sweater and a straw hat."

"No, I'm not," Bradford Mills grumbled.

"Then why did you dig up this old hat from your trunks?" Joyce demanded.

"As you can see, mom, it's just another day in Eden." Abby backed away from the feuding couple and went in to get some coffee. "I'm going to have to say goodbye now, mom. I promised Faith I'd get her some cake and I have Doyle with me," Abby said as she strode past another couple arguing.

Oddly enough, the heated discussion appeared to be about appropriate attire to wear for the picnic.

The charity event had been running for a couple of years. Joyce had been the one to suggest reviving an old tradition of auctioning picnic baskets to raise money for the local hospital but only after learning it had all started back in the 1920s. Inspired by the fashion of the time, she'd insisted everyone had to dress accordingly.

Abby was about to order her coffee when she saw the poster hanging behind the counter advertising the picnic.

Proper 1920s attire Non Optional.
No exceptions – for anyone.
That means you, Abby Maguire.

Abby looked down at Doyle. "Don't give me that doggy grin. If I have to dress up, then you have to dress up. We're in this together."

Doyle sighed.

Back at the Gazette, Abby found Faith busy at her computer, still grumbling about the possible scarcity of chocolate.

Faith looked up and pushed out a breath that spoke of frustration. "I'm going to have nightmares about this. All thanks to you."

"Cheer up. It might never happen." Abby set the

coffee and cake down. "Sorry to be the bearer of more bad news. Joyce beat you to it. She's already put up a poster for the picnic." Abby leaned against the desk. "Did you know proper attire for the picnic is non negotiable?"

"Of course. Everyone knows that. Including Bradford Mills."

"That's an odd remark to make."

Faith shook her head. "I just got off the phone with Eddie Faydon who told me she saw Joyce and Bradford arguing outside the café."

"I can't believe Eddie beat me to it. I saw them too." Like everyone who lived in Eden, the redheaded co-owner of the pub Abby had been staying at had her finger on the pulse. "It almost makes the Gazette redundant."

Faith sighed and took a bite of her cake. "Your scaremongering articles might take care of that."

Abby grabbed the digital camera from her desk and checked to make sure it had been charged.

"Kitty Belmont stored the props at the boat shed," Faith said. "We just need a photo of Kitty and her boyfriend, Gordon."

"Props?"

"A picnic basket. Kitty belongs to the Eden Thespians so she's also organized the costumes. Let's hope Gordon is a willing participant. She's super efficient and a bit of a control freak. I wouldn't be surprised if she's already set everything up for you."

Abby sipped her coffee. "How's the cake?"

Faith tilted her head in thought as she stared at her chocolate cake. "There's a strange aftertaste. I suspect this is what a last meal tastes like." She set her fork down. "It reminds me of the time the stores stopped stocking Delta Creams. They're an Australian version of Oreos. Suddenly, they disappeared from the shelves. I made my last cookie last for as long as I could, nibbling on it a bit at a time. When I got to the end, I wept."

"And?" Abby prodded. "Did the earth stop spinning on its axis?"

"A year later, I visited friends in the city and discovered they were back in store shelves right along with Oreos."

"All's well that ends well?"

Faith frowned. "I find scarcity stories scary and disturbing. They play havoc with my peace of mind."

Abby laughed under her breath. "Are we still friends?"

Faith took another bite of cake and gave her a toothy grin. "Of course. Now… go and bring back a fabulous photo and a new angle to promote the picnic that doesn't involve the extinction of chocolate."

Abby drove along the main street and wasn't surprised to see Joyce only now going back inside the café while Bradford Mills was striding back to his antique store, the straw hat in his hand.

"He doesn't look happy." Right on cue, Bradford

punched the air... with the hat. "I guess it could be worse." He might have used the hat as a punching bag. "Oh, to be in love."

Doyle sighed and rested his chin on his paws.

"Is that a 'wake me up when we get there' sigh? Don't get too comfortable. The lake isn't far." Only a five-minute drive away, almost within walking distance, Abby thought.

They left the township behind and, driving at a sedate pace, Abby took in the pretty scenery of the rolling hills and farms with the mountains as a backdrop.

The annual picnic had been rescheduled and brought forward a month. This had been Joyce Breeland's idea, saying everyone needed something to keep them busy.

"We need to heal," Abby said under her breath quoting Joyce.

This would be her first trip out to the lake. She'd been told there were several designated picnic areas for people who enjoyed swimming and boating. While it had comfortable amenities, it remained an exclusive spot for locals, only occasionally attracting tourists trekking out from the city.

Following the road sign, Abby made a turn into a winding road. "Okay, we're heading into the forest. Just thought you might want to know."

Doyle stirred and yawned in response.

"Not interested? I'm told we might encounter wombats." Doyle remained disinterested. "That's right, you're a local and I'm not. Well, let me tell you, there are no wombats in Seattle, but we do have rain." She leaned forward and peered up to catch a glimpse of the blue sky. "Do you realize it hasn't rained since I arrived? I'm almost beginning to miss it."

She wove her way through the forest until finally the road straightened. "There's a clearing up ahead." Slowing down, she caught the first glimpse of the lake. Then, she reached the picnic area entrance and had a full view of it. "Wow. It's actually bigger than I thought it would be." She drove in and parked next to another SUV. "Okay, this is it. Get ready to stretch your legs. Come on, no grumbling. You're an honorary reporter. You need to be ready to leap into action and catch that scoop."

Abby smiled. When she'd first arrived in Eden, Joyce Breeland had told her the locals liked to create their own excitement. Not much happened in a small town, so they had to make the best of it.

As a new arrival, Abby had become the main attraction, in a good way, Abby thought. She knew she'd been given a 'fair go'. Almost like a trial period to see how well she'd fit in.

So far, she'd managed to skate around any subject that might become controversial. From the start, she'd realized the Lamington saga would require delicate handling. Taking Joyce's lead, she'd remained impartial, sticking with facts and doing a write up about the history of the chocolate and coconut covered sponge cake without divulging her preferences. Although, secretly, she preferred the varieties with strawberry jam in the centre and she'd drooled over the ones with marmalade filling, a variety most purists frowned upon.

Living so far away from her friends and family would take some getting used to. However, the locals were making it easy for Abby. Everyone she'd met so far had been friendly and most had surprised her with their unique quirkiness and… kookiness.

"And these ones are no exception," Abby murmured as she spotted the couple who'd volunteered to pose for her photo.

They were both dressed in period costume from the 1920s. Kitty Belmont had an eggshell colored outfit. She'd matched a skirt cinched at the waist with a blouse with a sailor style collar. "That must have been a trend back in the day. I'm sure I heard Joyce describe her outfit in a similar way." Kitty also wore a cream colored hat shaped like a helmet, something else that had been quite fashionable at the time, Abby thought remembering seeing photos of her great grandmother wearing a similar hat.

Gordon Fisher looked quite comfortable in his cream trousers and sweater. Unlike Bradford, he didn't seem to have a problem with his straw hat.

Abby waved to them.

Kitty had set up the picnic blanket and basket on a light slope near the shore with a low hanging tree in the background.

"I thought this might be a good spot," Kitty called out. "Gordon tied a couple of boats to the tree. I hope you can get them in the shot."

"I'll do my best." Faith hadn't been wrong. Kitty was all efficiency.

"You'll have to tell me how to position my parasol so I don't block any of the pretty scenery. Gordon is about to strike a pose and look at me with adoring puppy eyes."

Without looking down at Doyle, Abby sensed him rolling his eyes. She watched as Kitty tucked her feet under her and sat primly, her back ramrod straight, while Gordon stretched out beside her, his head slightly tilted up as he gazed at Kitty with adoration.

"How's that?" Gordon asked.

Abby was about to answer, when the sound of another car pulling up drew everyone's attention.

"No. No. No." Kitty's exclamation struck like a lightning bolt. "How dared Miranda Hoppers show up here?"

Gordon tried to soothe her. "Calm down, Kitty. You don't want this to blow out of proportion."

"Calm down? Look at her. She's even wearing the same outfit I am. And who's that with her?"

"I don't recognize the gentleman," Gordon said.

Abby smiled at Gordon's tone. Hearing him fully embrace his role, she suspected he too belonged to the Eden Thespian theater group.

"An outsider. She's brought an outsider." Kitty surged to her feet and stormed toward the new arrivals.

Gordon mouthed an apology. "Kitty will have this sorted out in no time." He rose to his feet and strode toward Abby.

"I take it there's some sort of rivalry between them," Abby said.

"It's a McCoy/Hatfield feud," Gordon explained. "At least it's headed that way."

"With or without the mortality rate?" Abby asked.

"So far, there have only been shouting matches and snubs. Miranda Hoppers is a new Eden Thespian member. We have rules of precedence. As a founding member, Kitty retains first right of refusal for any leading role that comes up. Now Miranda is trying to undermine her authority… Excuse me, I think I need to break them up before it gets out of hand."

Abby stood back and watched the altercation unfold. Fingers were being pointed, parasols waved, but the two women were keeping an arm's length distance.

Losing interest, Doyle trotted off, his nose to the ground as he sniffed out new smells. Abby followed him along the shoreline toward the rowboats that had been tied up. "That looks like an expert sailor's knot. Gordon must have been a boy scout… or a sailor. I'm guessing boy scout." She took a couple of photos and managed to talk Doyle into hoping on. "Smile for the birdie." She laughed as Doyle lifted his chin and his paw. "Ahoy there. You look like a seasoned seafaring captain."

Looking into the distance, she saw houses on the opposite side of the lake. Someone had mentioned Eddie Faydon lived there with her fiancé. A compatriot, Abby thought and tried to recall which state he hailed from when a piercing screech broke her concentration.

"You poked me with your parasol. You all saw that. She poked me," Miranda yelled. "I will have you removed from the Eden Thespians. They will strip you bare and have you paraded along the main street…"

"Wow, talk about histrionics." Doyle shifted and leaned against Abby. "Yeah, she's scary. I thought Kitty's reputation preceded her, but Miranda is giving her a good run for her money." Abby raised her camera only to hesitate. "What do you think? Should I. This is a scoop of sorts. We could start a gossip column."

Doyle whimpered.

"No? You don't think I can compete with the Eden grapevine? Are you a betting dog?" She took a couple of extra shots, snatching one just as Kitty's parasol swooped through the air. "Priceless," Abby murmured. "And since we're the only witnesses, I think I stand a good chance of being first in with the news. How does Battle of the Thespians sound?"

CHAPTER 2

"The day of the picnic dawned bright and beautiful," Abby said as she strode into the Eden Rise Gazette office, her parasol in hand.

Faith's mouth gaped open. "Blimey! Get a hold of you."

Abby smiled. "What do you think of Doyle's little cap? It came from a teddy bear. It was the smallest I could find."

"I think it's cute, but going by Doyle's woeful expression, I'm thinking he doesn't share the sentiment."

"No, he grumbled all the way here."

"What's with the mincing steps?" Faith asked.

Abby put her foot forward. "My shoes are a size too big so I have to tread with care." She raised a monocle eyeglass to her eye. "You're looking splendid."

"I don't think I'll pass muster. The dress is too

loose. In the photos you took, Kitty's skirt looked tight around her waist."

"That's because Kitty didn't get it right. Her clothes are early 1900s. In the 20s, women did away with their corsets and the dress waistlines dropped. Are you ready?"

Faith nodded. "What's with the eyepiece?"

"I thought it might add character but I'm about to abandon the idea. The thing refuses to stay in place."

"I have to say, I'm surprised you went along with the whole dressing up rule."

Both Doyle and Abby looked at her. "Really? What do you think would happen if I'd turned up in regular clothes?"

Faith grinned. "Joyce Breeland would bar you from the café."

"That's right, and where would I be without her coffee?"

Faith shivered. "The thought is too scary to contemplate. I hope Joyce doesn't ever realize how much power she wields over all of us." Faith didn't bother locking the office door, something that still made Abby smile.

When Faith turned, her mouth gaped open again. "What on earth… Where did that come from?"

"This is an original 1920 convertible. I assume you know Charles Granger." The owner of Willoughby Park, a local deer farm, tipped his hat.

"We haven't been formally introduced," Faith said.

Abby did the honors.

"Ladies, your carriage… or rather, your touring car awaits you," Charles Granger said.

Abby clapped her hands. "Isn't it fabulous. Joyce is going to be green with envy."

"When did this become a competition?" Faith asked. Before Abby could answer, she raised a halting hand. "Just because she beat you to the scoop?"

Abby frowned. By the time she'd returned from taking the promotional photographs at the lake, news had already spread about Kitty and Miranda's exchange of harsh words.

How?

It should have been her scoop. She'd driven straight back to the Gazette and yet Joyce had already passed the information on to anyone who would listen.

"I'd like to put all that behind me, please." Abby made a breezy gesture with her hand. "I know this isn't a competition, but I believe I will win. Did I tell you Charles collects these beautiful cars?" She'd met him a few days before when she'd been expanding her horizons and scouting around the area to become better acquainted with her new stomping ground. Born in England, the eccentric landowner lived on a large estate a few miles outside of town and had introduced deer farming to the area.

Abby clapped her hands again. "I can't wait to see Joyce's face when we arrive."

Half an hour later, Faith turned to Abby. "When exactly are we going to arrive?"

They'd been chugging along the road at twenty miles an hour. If they'd been driving in a normal car, they would have arrived in five minutes.

"We'll make a grand entrance," Abby said.

Charles Granger tipped his hat at a car overtaking him.

"It sets a different pace," Abby remarked. "It's lovely to actually have the time to appreciate the scenery."

Faith chortled. "You've seen one cow, you've seen them all."

"Would you ladies like to listen to some music?" Charles asked. "It's a perk I had installed and I packed an old gramophone in the trunk."

The sounds of a jazz tune wafted around them. "The 1920s is known as both the Jazz Age and the Roaring Twenties," Abby said. "The older generation considered the music immoral and threatening to old cultural values which goes to show, very little has changed." Hugging Doyle against her, Abby leaned forward. "Did you know Jazz became known for including a lot of improvisation because the original jazz musicians couldn't read music?"

Faith shook her head. "I guess we're in for a detailed article."

Abby sat back and shrugged. "It helps to be thorough. At least I'm not killing off chocolate."

"So much for making a grand entrance. Where are you going to park the car, Charles?" The place was packed to capacity.

"No matter. I'll simply make my own space." He drove to the end of the gravel path and right onto the grass area. "I think everyone will see us now. We could even set up our picnic by the car. I'll take care of it."

"Wave," Abby said. "People are noticing us now."

Charles Granger hadn't been the only one to bring music along with him. Abby spotted a couple of gramophones with the most impressive one taking center stage at Joyce Breeland's picnic. The sounds of the early jazz era weaved around, mingling with the buzz of conversation and laughter.

Abby took out her camera and began taking snapshots. The entire town had turned up. She even noticed a few faces she didn't recognize and assumed they were people from the surrounding farms who rarely came into town because they normally worked from dawn to dusk.

She saw Kitty by the edge of the picnic grounds and took a photo of her. Scanning the grounds, she continued taking pictures. Moments later, Kitty appeared in another shot. Abby kept taking photos of her as she wove her way toward Gordon. They'd set up their picnic on the same spot they'd chosen for the promotional photographs. When Abby smiled at them, Gordon waved her over.

"Care for some champagne?" he offered.

"A sip would be lovely, thank you." Abby sat down on a plump cushion and gazed out across the lake. "All this makes me think of The Great Gatsby. I believe Jay Gatsby would have approved. Everyone looks sensational."

"Cucumber and lobster sandwich?" Kitty offered.

"Yes, please. What a treat."

"I placed a winning bid on a Joyce's Café basket. She donates a basket every year. Hers are always the best."

Abby nibbled on the delectable sandwich. "Is everyone here?" She specifically wanted to know about Miranda Hoppers but thought Kitty wouldn't appreciate being reminded.

"Everyone who matters," Kitty said, her lips pursing slightly as she adjusted her skirt. Appearing to find something wrong with it, she searched inside her small bag and continued adjusting her skirt.

Abby decided she needed to attend the next Eden Thespians rehearsal night. Sparks were bound to fly and she would get her scoop. She could sense something other than the mere exchange of words brewing between the two women.

When Abby saw Joyce Breeland meandering her way toward the flashy touring car, she excused herself.

She arrived just as Charles popped a champagne cork. Giving a small wave hello, she said, "Joyce. You look superb."

"So do you, Abby."

Abby smiled although Joyce's tone suggested she

knew something had been set into motion. A rivalry, perhaps? Abby decided to play it safe and offer a few more compliments as she twirled around. The cotton dress she'd selected in plain white had a tiny bow on the collar to match the one on her hat. The white shoes were a size too big for her but she'd been able to adjust the strap to keep them in place.

"This event would be nothing without you," Abby offered. "Faith told me how much money you raised last year. I'm sure you'll double it this year."

"Really?" Joyce's eyebrow curved up. "You brought your own basket. You're supposed to bid on one."

No, she hadn't brought a basket, but Charles had come fully prepared. "Oh… Yes, of course. We'll all be bidding." Abby shrugged. "Just as well Charles thought to bring one. It looks like we might have missed out."

"You haven't. There are still some left." Joyce leaned against the car. "By the way, nice touch. I wish I'd thought of it." She sent her gaze skipping around the picnic grounds. "I'm already tweaking the event for next year. I think we should have it at twilight and set a Great Gatsby theme with formal wear. Tuxedos for the gentlemen and evening gowns for the ladies. I'm picturing Chinese lanterns and… Oh, it'll come to me."

Abby bit her lip. She could have kicked herself. She'd only just been entertaining a similar thought. Once again, Joyce had managed to beat her to it. Abby wondered if she'd also considered hiring a live band. That would be a splendid idea. She savored the words and could imagine Joyce giving one of her rare smiles that suggested they were on the same wavelength. Yes, a live band with everyone wearing cream colored tuxedos.

Charles handed the champagne glasses around. "You could also hire a live jazz band."

Joyce frowned. "Why didn't I think of that? Thank you Charles. You're a treasure."

Faith sidled up to Abby and whispered, "I think you're trying too hard and it's showing."

Abby whispered back, "I thought of the live band idea and was about to tell her when Charles beat me to it."

"What's going on with you?" Faith asked.

Abby pursed her lips.

"Is this still about Joyce beating you with the scoop about Kitty and Miranda?"

"No," Abby huffed out.

"I think it is. I had no idea you were so competitive."

"I'm not. It's just that…"

Faith grinned. "You can't stand it when someone beats you at your own game?"

Abby lifted her chin. "You're forgetting about our mode of transportation. No one else thought of doing that."

"Let's hope it doesn't rain," Faith murmured.

"I'm going to place bids on our basket." Or else, she'd never hear the end of it. Moments later, she returned carrying a basket.

"That was quick work," Faith said.

"Yes, well… This was the last one."

"Which one did you get?" Joyce asked.

Abby looked at the label. "The Queen Alexandra." Whatever that meant. Strawberries and cream came to mind. Lobster sandwiches. A quiche or a terrine fit for a queen...

Joyce smiled. "Oh, I nearly placed a bid on that one. It's Harriet Newton's special."

That sounded promising.

Joyce tilted her head. "It's strange. I would never have picked you for a pickled tongue sandwich type of person."

Pickled what?

The edge of Joyce's lip kicked up. Abby must have looked sufficiently lost for words because Joyce went on to explain, "Queen Alexandra's favorite finger sandwich. Mustard butter, watercress and ox tongue."

Pickled. Ox. Tongue.

Joyce's eyes brimmed with amusement. "You know, offal."

"Offal?"

"The entrails and internal organs of animals. I'm partial to liver because I like pâté but it has to be goose liver. Although, I've become sensitive about the poor geese's plight. So I haven't had it in ages." Abby's raised eyebrows prompted Joyce to add, "I don't care for the practice of force-feeding them."

But she was okay with ox tongue. Pickled ox tongue.

"Well, dig in," Joyce said.

Okay, so she'd grown up in a semi-rural environment, but her mom was a vegetarian and while she'd made sure Abby had a balanced diet growing up, she had omitted to introduce her to... unique dining.

"I might keep it for dinner. I've already had some of Kitty's lobster sandwiches." And Abby wished she'd helped herself to more.

"Oh, yes. Kitty Belmont won my basket. This year I donated three." Joyce patted the car. "If you'd been here earlier, you might have picked one up."

Meaning... she could have been enjoying lobster sandwiches instead of pickled tongue. "I should mingle. Otherwise, I won't have a story to write."

Doyle appeared to have a keen eye for detail. Wherever he stopped, Abby found a great photo opportunity. "Doyle, you're officially my star cub reporter."

A few people had ventured out to the lake on boats; the women twirling their parasols while the men rolled up their sleeves and made the job of rowing look easier than it surely was.

Abby held her hand up to shield her eyes from the sun. She counted a dozen boats. Her gaze skipped from one boat to the other. Narrowing her eyes, she noticed one didn't have anyone on-board. It was out in the middle of the lake and gently moving toward the shore.

Doyle came to sit beside her. "Does that look like fun to you?"

Yawning, he looked away.

"Okay, point the way. I need to have a decent stock of photos to show Faith." To her amusement, children appeared to have abandoned their electronic gadgets in favor of the simple pleasure of hoops. "I bet anything the novelty will wear off in no time." Although, they did appear to be more cheerful.

Abby made the rounds, stopping to chat to people. Along the way, she found a couple with a Joyce Breeland basket but they'd already scoffed all the delicious sandwiches. It took her half an hour to find the other basket, but she was again out of luck as it sat empty of all sandwiches.

Strolling back to the shore, Abby looked down in time to see Doyle pawing at his cap. "All right. I'll put you out of your misery." Stooping down, she removed the cap and gave him a scratch and some well-earned praise for being so well behaved. As she looked up, she caught sight of a boat disappearing behind an over-hanging tree. "I think someone is looking for a secluded spot." And there were quite a few around the shoreline, with little coves sheltered by trees and bushes. Yes, Abby thought, they're definitely looking for some privacy. Most of the people going out on the water appeared intent on reaching the middle of the lake before turning back.

Doyle sniffed around the bushes and was about to disappear when Abby called him back. "I don't want you wandering off. There's too much going on here. You need to stay by my side." She laughed. "Just listen to me. I sound like a mother hen."

Looking over his shoulder at the bushes, Doyle whimpered lightly. Huffing his intention to disobey Abby, he took a step toward the bushes.

"No, Doyle. I mean it. You stay with me."

"Abby."

Abby turned and saw Faith waving to her.

"The sandwiches are fast disappearing. Come back before they're all gone."

Abby grinned. "Faith sure knows how to entice me... Not." She waved back. "Come on, Doyle. We should at least pretend. Otherwise, Joyce will catch on."

She strode past Kitty and Gordon and wished they'd ask her to join them but they were busy singing along to a 1920s love ballad playing on their gramophone. Abby guessed Bradford Mills had made a killing selling gramophones and old vinyl records.

"Charles has some smoked salmon sandwiches," Faith said, "I'm afraid he ate all your pickled tongue ones."

"Oh, Charles. How could you?" Abby asked, her tone mocking.

"I know a lady in distress when I see one," he said. "Offal isn't for everyone. Lucky me, I acquired a taste for it at boarding school in England. The cook was eventually caught pilfering funds. She used to buy the cheapest cuts of meat for us boys and squirreled away the savings for herself."

Abby reached for her bag and drew out a small bowl for Doyle. Grabbing a bottle of water, she tipped the contents inside. "Don't look at me with that woeful expression. You've had your meal." She waited a few minutes and then brought out a doggy biscuit. "One and only one. The vet warned me not to overfeed you."

As Abby settled back to nibble on her delectable sandwich, she searched the picnic grounds for Miranda Hoppers and her partner. She hadn't come across as the type to back down and Abby expected her to make some sort of public nuisance of herself.

Couples were now finishing their lunches and getting up to stroll around the lake. Some of the rowboats were heading back to shore while others were setting off.

When she finished her sandwich, Abby drew out her cell phone and called her mom. Looking at Faith, she said, "I know, I've already spoken with her this week but if I don't do a video chat and show her the picnic and everyone dressed up, she'll never forgive me."

She started out by showing off the car and then she introduced her mom to Charles. Her mom insisted she make the rounds and show her everything and everyone.

"Where did they all get their costumes from?" her mom asked.

"I raided the local theater group and I'm sure some people have trunks of old clothes stored away."

"Yes, of course. I still have some of your great grandmother's clothes, including her wedding gown, if you ever want to try it on."

"Really? You never offered before."

"I'd forgotten about it. It's been years since I looked

at it. I should air it out and make sure the moths haven't feasted on it."

Abby turned the cell phone and showed her mom the lake.

"I'd almost believe you've time traveled. Everyone's done such a wonderful job of recreating the era. And look at those boats. Someone must take great care of them. They look like antiques. Are those houses in the distance? Can you move closer or zoom in?"

"Sorry, I haven't mastered the art of walking on water and… Mom, this is a cell phone not a proper camera." Nevertheless, she moved as close as she could to the shore without getting her shoes wet. They needed to go back to the props department without any scuff marks.

Looking around, she spotted the rowboat that had drifted off behind some trees. "I don't have it in me to go for that scoop," Abby murmured. She needed some sort of newsworthy item. If not a scoop, at least a bit of gossip she could exchange with Joyce. Her friendship couldn't be all take and no give. So far, Joyce had been the one to convey information…

"What did you say? I missed it," her mom said.

"I'm… I'm off my game. I need a newsworthy snippet or something of interest because…" She supposed she could say her reputation hung in the balance. Although, her job in uncovering the person responsible for Dermot Cavendish's death should give her a good standing in the community for years to come.

Seeing Joyce Breeland heading toward the shore,

Abby frowned. Another couple of steps and Joyce would see the boat hiding behind the trees. Knowing her, she'd even be able to identify the occupants. Abby had to distract her.

"What's going on? Why are you pointing the phone at the ground? Is there something you don't want me to see? Abby, are you there?"

Hearing her mom's voice, Joyce turned.

"Tell Joyce I'm waving," her mom said.

Abby waved the cell phone at Joyce. "Hey, aren't you going out on a rowboat?"

"I want to," Joyce said. "But everyone's staying out longer and longer. I told them they were only allowed to row to the middle of the lake and then back so everyone could have a go." She hitched her thumb over her shoulder. "And someone looks like they've found a secluded spot. I included a note on the posters. There are children present, so no funny business."

"I saw the boat drift toward the shore a while ago," Abby said and felt a rush of heat settling on her cheeks. What had come over her? She'd never been in competition with anyone. In fact, she'd avoided sports all her life because she simply didn't have it in her to prove herself better than someone else.

Joyce clambered up the slope.

"Hey, where are you going?" Abby followed her.

"There's a path winding down to that part of the lake. When people stopped being able to follow the shoreline around the lake, they started trekking back up and around. Eventually, they wore out a path. It would have been easier to cut back the trees, but half the town is against it, saying there's been enough felling and it has to stop."

"Abby? Are you huffing?" her mom asked. "I think you're out of shape."

"It's my shoes. I need to take care I don't scratch them and that makes walking more difficult." Although, Abby had to admit it wouldn't hurt to get some more daily exercise. Maybe she could suggest a walking club…

"You should set up a walking club," her mom suggested. "Make sure you stay in shape because after a certain age, there's simply no getting rid of the excess weight."

"I don't have a weight problem. Mom, I'm going to call you back later on."

"No, don't you dare disconnect me. I need to see what happens next."

"What do you mean?"

"Well, it's obvious you two want to surprise the couple on the boat."

"Mom, isn't it late for you?"

"Of course it is. It's close to midnight over here. But this is better than staying up to watch a favorite movie. I think I see the boat. Please try to hold the phone steady."

Great. Now her mom was one step ahead of her too. Abby turned the cell phone to face her.

"Oh, dear. Why are you frowning?" her mom asked.

Looking ahead, Abby's eyebrows hitched up.

"What am I missing? Quick. Point the cell phone in the right direction," her mom hollered.

The boat was bumping against the shore and someone was in it. "Um, Joyce. I don't think we should go any further. We might be interrupting something—" Abby frowned again. She could see the rowboat moving but not the person inside the boat.

Joyce must have reached the same conclusion because she came to a sudden stop and said, "I don't like the look of this."

"Abby. What's going on?" her mom asked.

Doyle ran up and leaped over a thick bush.

A couple of more steps brought them up to the edge of the track. Beyond that, there was a strip of thick shrubbery but they could see the boat clearly now.

Doyle leaped over a large branch, disappeared into the bushes and then emerged again. He tried to scramble onto the boat but his little legs weren't long enough.

Abby stood on tiptoes and craned her neck. "That's a woman inside, and she's alone." And not moving. Her heart gave an alarming thump against her chest. "I'll call you later, mom." Abby didn't wait for a response. She disconnected the call and, drawing in a deep breath, she called Detective Inspector Joshua Ryan.

CHAPTER 3

*A*fter raising the alarm with the police, Joyce
helped Abby scramble her way to the boat.

"We have to make sure," Abby said. "She might
have fainted from sunstroke. Or… or she might have
had one too many glasses of champagne." Belatedly,
Abby wished she hadn't jumped to conclusions and
called the police.

What if this turned out to be a big
misunderstanding?

She hoped that was the case.

It took some careful maneuvering to move through
the thick undergrowth. Along the way, her shoe slipped
off. Bending down to pick it up, she heard a tear…

"The Eden Thespians wardrobe department is going
to give me an earful."

Reaching the boat, Abby tried to ease her breathing,
but it didn't work.

Her shoulders tightened, her hands shook. She had

to do this. Leaning into the boat, relief seeped through her. She'd expected to be confronted with a face looking up.

"Hello," Abby said even though a part of her didn't expect to hear a response. She patted the woman on the back and then gave her a light shake. Again, no response. Finally, she checked for a pulse. She tried the woman's neck and then her wrist and then her neck again.

No pulse. And worse…

She felt cold.

Abby scrambled back. "I couldn't pick up a pulse and she feels cold." Stone cold and stiff. "She's facing down so I can't tell if the lips are blue and, no, I didn't recognize her. Not from the back. I can only say the clothes confirm she'd been attending the picnic."

Joyce bit the edge of her lip and gave a stiff nod. "What do we do now?"

"Call the ambulance." Abby knew the operator would guide her through the procedure and help her to check again for a pulse. When she'd called Joshua, he'd told her to hang tight as the ambulance was already on its way but it wouldn't hurt to talk with an operator. They were trained to deal with these types of situations giving first aid guidance and… support. Abby's breath hitched. She definitely needed support.

Abby circled back to the car, taking the long way

around and back along the shoreline, along the way taking as many photos as she could.

Joyce had first hurried off to get her fiancé, Bradford, and Charles to stand guard over the boat thinking that if they'd stumbled onto the scene then someone else could too and that was definitely something they wished to avoid.

Bradford and Charles had then checked her vital signs and found none.

While Abby had followed the path down to the shoreline, Joyce had taken off in the opposite direction covering the higher ground where the cars were parked. She had retrieved her cell phone so between them they should have accumulated enough photographs to account for everyone attending the picnic.

"Smart thinking," Joyce said as she joined Abby. "We'll at least be able to place most people."

And thank goodness for that. Once everyone realized what had happened, panic would set in.

Doyle stood by at attention, almost as if he sensed the imminent arrival of the police.

"Let's go back to the boat," Joyce suggested.

"You go. I'll stay and wait for Joshua... I mean, the police. Someone will need to show them the way." Abby had called Joshua on his direct number, but she had no idea what the protocol would be. She only assumed he would come himself, but for all she knew, he might have sent someone else.

She'd called him a second time and when she'd spoken with him, she'd remained calm but her voice had sounded strained. Luckily, Joshua hadn't asked too many questions. In any case, she'd only been able to give him basic information.

A woman. A boat. No pulse.

Abby gave a slow shake of her head. Maybe he'd wanted to ask questions but had sensed Abby's tension and shock.

Joyce pushed out a hard breath. "I'm glad someone has remained calm and is thinking straight."

Abby didn't mention the slight trembling she felt inside her. "Thank you but you're holding yourself together admirably well too." And thank goodness for that. Anyone else might have taken off at a run screaming. "Hang on. Do you have any idea how we'll manage all these people? I'm afraid someone will pick up on my vibes and know something's happened and then, who knows what they'll do." Curiosity seekers might want to take a closer look. At the very least, people would ask questions and expect answers.

"I think the police can take care of crowd control," Joyce offered. "We really only need to make sure no one wanders toward the rowboat or tramples on footprints." Joyce slapped her hand to her cheek. "I guess we've already done that."

Abby supposed the police could work on a process of elimination. "We had no choice and we didn't know what we were about to find."

While Joyce returned to the boat, Abby remained by the car, thinking she needed to focus on pretending nothing had happened, at least until the police arrived. If she didn't stop fidgeting soon someone would start getting suspicious. That remained her most pressing concern.

Abby made eye contact with Eddie Faydon who smiled and waved. She guessed the man sitting with the pub's co-owner was her fiancé.

"Be calm. Be cool. Wave back and pray she doesn't come over." Abby didn't think she'd be able to restrain herself.

Looking around, she didn't noticed Mitch Faydon. Abby guessed he'd had to stay back at the pub to work. She turned her attention to making a list of people she'd assumed would come, but hadn't. Markus Faydon and Hannah Melville both worked at the pub. Pete Cummins, the vet… Well, she'd heard say he worked all year round and was on call twenty-four hours a day.

There really weren't that many people who hadn't come, which meant they had the vast majority of locals attending the picnic.

If this turned out to be something other than a death by natural causes, then…

"Where's your mind going with this?" Abby whispered under her breath. "Interesting question. If, and this is a big if, it turns out to be a suspicious death, there'll be a lot of suspects."

How had the woman died and why hadn't anyone noticed? She had to have come with someone, and that someone should have noticed her missing.

Abby shook her head. She needed to stop thinking about it.

"Have some water, Doyle. And I'll give you another biscuit. It might be a while before we get home."

Doyle looked around and then appeared to relax. Abby drew out a doggie biscuit for him. He sniffed it and looked away. "Not interested?" Bending down, she gave him a pat on the rump. "I think you knew there was something wrong when you went sniffing around the bushes. Sorry I pulled you away. Next time—" Heavens. Next time?

"Hey, there you are." Faith strode up to them, her eyes bright and her smile wide. "I don't remember the picnic being this good last year. I hope you took lots of photos. It would be nice to put together a commemorative album." Faith looked around. "Where's Charles?"

Abby sighed and, making sure no one would hear her, she told Faith everything that had happened. It took a moment for Faith to react to the news.

"Next time, you might want to start by suggesting I sit down first," Faith said. "My legs are wobbling and look at my hands. They're shaking."

"I hope there isn't a next time," Abby said. "This is meant to be a quiet little town."

"I feel I should apologize. In fact, on behalf of everyone, I'm sorry." Faith pressed her hand to her heart. "Heavens. My heart is pumping hard against my chest. Who could it be?"

Abby's gaze skipped around the picnic area. She had a vague idea but didn't want to say for fear that she might be wrong.

Hearing the crunch of tires on gravel, she turned.

"Joshua." She'd met the detective the first day she'd arrived in Eden. Abby remembered he'd given her a coffee from Joyce's Café and had set her off on a road to absolute addiction to Joyce's brew.

A few heads turned his way but everyone resumed what they were doing. He hadn't come alone. Nodding, he introduced Detective Inspector Quentin McNamara.

Both detectives cast their eyes over the picnic area and then Joshua got on the phone to give the police the go-ahead.

Apparently, Joshua had played it safe.

"Did you think my phone call was a crank?"

"Not at all. I just didn't want the squad cars to drive in with the sirens blaring. It would have set everyone on a panic."

"Like in the movie Jaws," Faith said.

"The police are going to arrive now and cordon off the area. Can you show me where you found the body?"

Abby leaned in. "Everyone knows something's happened. I'm guessing they'll follow."

"Let's stay calm. As far as anyone knows, I'm only here to have a chat with you. They're not mind readers."

"Joshua… Your clothes are a dead giveaway. You're here on official business."

Both detectives wore denim jeans and sports jackets and had a hands on hips look about them that spoke of serious police business.

"What's wrong with what I'm wearing?"

"It's not white… or even eggshell white."

"I suppose you're right," Joshua said.

Abby could see everyone sitting up and straining to catch a snippet of conversation so they could add two and two together. Even the people who'd gone out into the lake had noticed something happening. The rowboats had all come to a stop, and some picnickers were making their way back to shore.

"All right. Quentin will stay here with Faith." He bent down and gave Doyle a scratch behind the ears. "Is this casual enough for you?"

Abby nodded.

Straightening, Joshua nudged her arm. "Let's just walk nice and easy. Pretend we're going for a stroll. Which way?"

She signaled with her eyes.

"Tell me how you found the body."

Abby tried to piece together the events but had to double back a couple of times to get the sequence right.

"Do you have any other useful information?" Joshua asked.

"She felt cold to the touch and now that I think about it, she also felt stiff. How long does it take for rigor mortis to set in?"

"As soon as four hours."

Four hours… That would place the time of death at roughly the same time people had begun arriving. "I noticed something else." Abby tapped her chin. "It might be nothing but I get the feeling she slumped over." And there had been something else…

"What?" Joshua asked, almost as if he'd read her mind.

"I saw something but, what with calling you and checking for a pulse..." She shook her head. "This might come as a surprise, but I'm not used to seeing dead bodies. Give me a minute, it'll come to me." Her cell phone rang. "My mom. She'll want to know what's happening."

"Why? Did you call her?"

"No, I'd been talking on the phone with her. Actually, we were video chatting, when we noticed something odd about the rowboat and I only disconnected the call when I rang you."

"You should answer," Joshua suggested.

"Mom, I'm fine. Joshua's here and... I can't talk now." She turned the phone to face Joshua who smiled and waved at her mom.

"Everything is under control, Eleanor. No need to worry." Joshua's eyes widened slightly.

Abby looked at the screen. "Mom. Did you just scowl at Joshua? This isn't his fault." Promising to ring back with an update, she ended the call. "Sorry. My mom has expressive eyebrows. She can bring a room to a standstill with her look of disapproval. But she's really quite nice."

They made their way toward the path as discreetly as they could. When they reached the boat, Joshua gestured for her to stand back.

"You're kidding. I'm the one who discovered the body." Abby swallowed. Her heart thumped all the way up to her throat.

"Are you all right?"

She gave a stiff nod but that only made her realize how light-headed she felt.

"Stay here. I need to get to the boat."

She watched Joshua make his way through the thick undergrowth.

Charles, Bradford and Joyce had stepped back from the boat but only after securing it to a branch with a rope.

Joyce hugged herself and gave Abby a small smile. "This is dreadful. I'm glad you had the courage to feel for a pulse. I don't think I would have been able to do it."

"You'd be surprised what you can do when you absolutely have to do something." Abby craned her neck for a better look. "I just remembered something. The oars. They're not there."

Joshua returned, his cell phone pressed to his ear.

Abby heard him passing some information to the ambulance officers. When he finished his call, he turned to the others and asked if they could stay a while longer.

Taking Abby by the arm, he guided her back to the clearing. Joshua gave Abby a brisk smile and looked away. "Okay, here they are."

"How is the police going to contain the situation without alarming everyone?"

"It's what they're trained to do." Joshua shook his head. "I don't think anyone will drive off without first finding out as much as they can. Although, people with children will probably want to set a safe distance."

"I'm sure she didn't come alone. Surely someone is going to realize they're missing a partner."

His cell phone rang.

Abby watched him but couldn't read his expression.

"The ambulance is less than five minutes away. They were delayed on another emergency call. It's been one of those days. We need to clear out everyone with small children now. There's no need to expose them…"

To a body bag, Abby thought.

"You could say someone's fallen ill."

He nodded. "Good idea."

In an ideal world, everyone would have gone home but no one actually believed the story about someone falling ill. There were simply too many police officers for that story to stick. Curiosity and a sense of rising dread kept most people lingering at the picnic grounds even after the police had assured them there was nothing to see.

Abby wondered if the police really expected people to buy into the assurance or if they assumed the message carried an underlying threat. Cross the line and you'll suffer the consequences.

Luckily, everyone with children agreed they needed to spare them the experience. While most lived in farms and were used to the harsh realities of life, some aspects were best avoided.

"What's going on?" Abby heard someone ask. A few people started making a beeline for her as if guided by a sixth sense toward the one person they assumed would have access to privileged information.

Any minute now she expected to be mobbed but then Joshua strode up to her. "You should go home, Abby."

Abby didn't want to argue with him, but that didn't mean she'd go away. She had a job to do.

People stood back watching in silence. A forensic team had been called in and they swept the area. Standing back from the immediate scene, Abby couldn't tell what else was happening. With the police in full control now, Joyce and the others had been guided away from what everyone suspected had now become a crime scene.

"Can we expect a statement from the police?" Charles asked.

Everyone turned to Abby and she turned to look at Joshua, her eyebrow cocked. "Do you wish to make a statement?"

"Cause of death hasn't been determined yet," Joshua said.

Joyce cleared her throat. "Did you see anything that might lead you to suspect foul play?" When Joshua didn't answer, Joyce nudged Abby and said, "I'm not the press. You ask him."

"Joshua, could I have a word in private, please?" Abby strode away from the group.

Joshua folded his arms. "I can't give you information I don't have, Abby."

"It's getting late. People need to have something to

take away with them. You need to give them some sort of assurance... something to set their minds at ease."

"Don't you think I know that?" He brushed his hand across his brow. "It would help if we could identify the victim. We were expecting someone to approach us, worried they're missing a companion, but so far, no one's come forth." He looked toward Joyce and lowered his voice. "Do you think she'd be up to it? She knows everyone in town."

"Joyce is a tough cookie and I'm sure she'll be only too happy to assist. You might want to mention something about her discretion and thank her for helping to keep the area free of stragglers."

Joshua waited a good ten seconds before answering. "Thank you for the prompt."

Abby took Joyce aside. "Joyce, are you up to identifying the victim?" All color drained from her cheeks. "Sorry to put you on the spot. I'll come with you. Oh, and we have to keep the information to ourselves until the next of kin is informed."

"That goes without saying." Joyce lowered her head as if in thought. "Am I going to have nightmares? I imagine I will."

"Yeah, you probably will."

Regardless, Joyce began making her way toward the path with Bradford by her side and Charles following behind.

The body hadn't been removed yet but as they drew closer to the little cove, Abby could see the victim had been placed on a stretcher.

Of all the places to have died, Abby thought, why did it have to be here and now?

Prompted by Joshua who drew the zipper on the body bag open, Joyce stepped forward.

For a moment, she looked reluctant.

Abby stepped up to her and gave her a reassuring hug.

Joyce's shoulders lifted and dropped. "Okay. I can do this." She looked down.

Standing beside her, Abby looked down too.

They both gasped.

"Miranda. It's Miranda Hoppers."

"Are you sure?" Joshua asked.

Joyce gave a stiff nod while Abby sighed and closed her eyes, although that did nothing to erase the image of Miranda's face from her mind.

Joyce grabbed her hand and tugged her away. "I have a flask of brandy in my basket."

"Good thinking." Abby pinched her cheeks. "I'm sure I'm looking as pale as a ghost."

Joyce brushed her hand across her face. "Did she… Did she look bloated to you?"

"Ugh, I wish you hadn't mentioned the bloating. Now the image won't budge from my mind."

"And her lips looked puffy." Joyce shook her head. "I am not going to get any sleep tonight."

Abby agreed and she also thought a shot of brandy wouldn't go far enough. She wanted oblivion. "I'm going to have to find a way to bleach my memory."

CHAPTER 4

*a*fter waving Charles off, Abby and Faith hitched a ride back to town with Joyce and Bradford. For the first time since arriving in Eden, no one talked. Not even Faith who preferred to work through anything bothering her out loud.

Bradford pulled up outside the pub where Abby had been staying. They all looked at one another and, again, didn't say anything.

Abby had to force herself to move her lips. "I'll see you all… tomorrow." Doyle trotted ahead of her, almost looking weary. "I guess you missed your snooze time. Sorry."

She saw Mitch Faydon at the bar with a group of people huddled together. Seeing her, Mitch straightened.

"Is it true?" he asked.

Abby chortled. Her reaction caught her by surprise and then she remembered Mitch asking the same question soon after Abby had arrived in Eden and Faith answering 'Yes, it's true, the earth is round.'

Nodding, she lifted her hand to tuck her hair behind her ear and belatedly remembered she still wore a hat.

Mitch leaned against the bar. "Eddie called a while ago to say the lake was a hive of activity with police swarming the place."

Everyone at the bar turned to Abby.

Doyle trotted on ahead, reached the stairs and looked back at her.

She gave Mitch a brief, stilted rundown.

"That's the same information Eddie had," he said, "I'd hoped you'd be able to throw in a name."

Abby sighed. "You know the drill. The police need to contact the next of kin." Abby looked at the group and prayed there were no next of kin among them.

"So you have a name, but you can't share it with us."

Doyle whimpered. "Sorry, I… I have a story to write and Doyle is in desperate need of a snooze." It seemed they both were. The moment Abby sat on her couch she slumped sideways and promptly fell asleep.

A while later she nearly rolled off the couch. "I'm a lifestyle reporter," she groaned. Before she could fully wake up, her cell phone rang. She answered in a slurred tone.

"What's wrong with you?" Faith asked. "Have you hit the bottle?"

"I get the feeling I don't respond well to death." Shortly after discovering Dermot Cavendish's body, she had collapsed on her bed and had fallen asleep. "I fell asleep."

"Narcolepsy."

"Huh?"

"Daytime sleepiness can be brought on by stress," Faith explained. "I had an aunt who constantly worried. Every bit of bad news made her drowsy. She used to spend her days taking naps. Finally, she had to stop watching the news."

Abby surged to her feet. She couldn't become that type of person. She needed to stay alert and... and on the job 24/7. "So what's up, Faith? Why did you call?"

"I assumed you were going to work on your story. I wondered if maybe you wanted some company. I could be your sounding board."

"Yeah, sure. Come over."

A knock at the door had Abby swinging around. "Is that you?"

"Yes."

And she hadn't come alone. Joyce stood behind Faith.

Smiling, Joyce held up a tray. "I brought coffee." She'd changed out of her pretty 1920s ensemble switching over to a film noire persona, her black top and black tights matched with a mid-thigh length trench coat and a black beret.

Faith set a large bag on the small dining table and drew out a couple of large notebooks. "I thought these might come in handy." She looked around the apartment. "We could tape notes on the wall."

Abby must have looked sufficiently mystified because Faith added, "I thought you might want to start piecing together the events."

"How about we start with the coffee," Abby suggested and gestured toward the couch. "Make yourselves comfortable."

Along with the coffee, Joyce had also brought a selection of pastries. "Just in case you need a hit of sugar. I find it helps to generate ideas." Joyce shrugged. "Faith told me how you two drew up a timeline for Dermot's case."

Case? "I'm a reporter not a P.I."

"Be that as it may, we all know Detective Joshua Ryan is not going to share information with us. Since we were the first on the scene, I think we can do a good job of piecing together some vital information." Joyce took a sip of her coffee. "Also, you were at the picnic site for the photo shoot and you witnessed an altercation between Miranda Hoppers and Kitty Belmont."

"Yes, about that… How did you find out about it?" By the time Abby had returned to town, news about the altercation had already spread, beating her at her own game.

"I have my ways." Joyce shrugged. "And, no, I won't reveal my sources."

There'd only been four people to witness the exchange, five if she included herself. Abby narrowed it down to Kitty Belmont.

"Are you about to suggest Kitty killed Miranda?" Abby asked.

Joyce quirked her eyebrow. "It's a possibility. Let's face it, they have been at it for ages."

Too obvious, Abby thought. If Kitty wanted to get rid of Miranda, she would not have been so open about her hostility toward her. Shaking her head, Abby helped herself to a coffee.

"I'll get the ball rolling." Faith uncapped a sharpie pen and wrote Miranda's name. Tearing the page off, she stuck it on the wall. "This would be easier with a whiteboard but I get the feeling you're not up to going to the office."

Abby shook her head and then nodded.

"Exactly. You don't know if you're coming or going. That's why we came to you."

Abby's voice hitched. "You conspired to push me into action?"

Joyce offered her a pastry. "Let's get some sugar into you and if that doesn't help, I'm sure Mitch will be only too happy to provide some room service. Hannah could whip you up an egg white omelet."

Doyle stirred awake and stretched.

"Feeling better?" Abby asked him. He meandered over to her and pressed his nose against her leg. "I think he wants to go out. I'm not sure. He's still training me to read the signs. I won't be long."

"All right," Joyce said. "But I'm warning you. We're not going anywhere."

Abby used the opportunity to snap out of whatever had taken a hold of her. As a lifestyle reporter, she didn't have front-line experience, so her exposure to crime, violence and... dead bodies remained limited.

She avoided the pub's main entrance and instead used the narrow stairs leading down to the residents' entrance.

Doyle sniffed his way to his favorite tree. When he lifted his leg to do his business, Abby turned and gave him some privacy.

A car drove by. Abby saw the driver and passenger wearing cream-colored clothes. When Abby and her group had finally left the picnic area, there had only been a handful of people lingering and looking lost. Shock could do that to people. An unexpected event could turn their brains into mush, with the smallest decision becoming an insurmountable task.

She could imagine everyone's dinner table conversation. It would be muted. Stilted. Awkward and full of avoidance.

Pass the salt, please.

How's the lamb? Not too pink, I hope...

This wine is perfect. Remind me to get some more.

Everyone would avert their gazes. Then someone would lift their eyes and they'd make eye contact with someone else at the table and they'd engage in a wordless conversation.

Finally, someone would blurt out a remark about what they'd seen that day and that would set the floodgates open.

Can you believe what happened?

I wonder how and… who could it be? And what if it wasn't an accident?

Suddenly, the chatter would become lively but, if there were children in the house, the tones would remain hushed.

Doyle returned to her side and sat down.

"Don't get too comfortable. We have to go back inside. They're expecting us." Abby heard someone step out of the pub.

Mitch strode up to her saying, "I saw Joyce and Faith going up to your apartment. What are you girls up to?"

Abby put her hands up. "Caught red-handed. We're sneaking boys in."

Mitch didn't smile. "I know you know something and you've been asked not to say anything."

"That sounds like a tongue twister." Abby looked down at Doyle who shifted and looked away. "Once I get the go-ahead, I promise you'll be the first to know. Sorry, it's this next of kin business."

"If you girls decide to pull an all-nighter, let me know and I'll bring up some food."

Abby gave him a small salute and went back inside. When she strode into her apartment, she found Joyce and Faith facing the wall. Half of it had already been covered with notes.

Joyce stepped back. "Good, you're here just in time to provide some essential information. I'll ask a few pertinent questions and—"

Abby beat her to it. "Did Miranda have family living in the area?"

"No. Faith and I were just discussing that. As far as I know, Miranda Hoppers was an only child. As for her parents..." Joyce shrugged. "She never mentioned them."

"Only child? How do you know that?" Abby asked.

"The café is my information pipeline. For the record, I don't go out of my way to eavesdrop on people's conversations. I overheard the Eden Thespians talking about siblings and Miranda mentioned she didn't have any."

"How long had she lived in Eden?"

Joyce looked at Faith as if to confer with her. "A little over a year."

Faith nodded. "She purchased that pretty farmhouse with a creek running through her property. It's near the lake. Shortly after moving in, she set tongues wagging when she installed a hot tub in her back garden and surrounded it with statues of naked women."

Joyce smiled. "You should take note, Abby. As a new resident, you need to walk a straight and narrow path. Don't do anything to draw attention to yourself."

"Okay. I won't install a Jacuzzi ... in my apartment." Abby frowned. "Hang on. I thought I was supposed to embrace the absurd."

Faith looked at Joyce. "What is she talking about?"

"I've no idea." Joyce picked up her coffee and strode around the apartment. "She might be having a go at our 'unique' way of doing things."

Abby wanted to ask Joyce to explain her understanding of the word 'unique'. She'd never met anyone so devoted to the idea. Her dress style, her mannerisms… it all pointed to an obsession with standing out in a crowd.

Abby shook her head. "Back to Miranda Hoppers."

Joyce sat down. "Yes, poor Miranda. I can't believe she's dead. Who'd want to kill her?" Joyce raised her hand. "Yes, I know. The cause of death hasn't been determined yet, but I am willing to bet a year's supply of free coffee someone killed her. Any takers?"

Faith chortled. "Even without hearing the official verdict from the police, I think we're all prepared to assume someone killed her."

Abby cleared her throat. "What did she do for a living?"

"Miranda Hoppers didn't work." Joyce tapped her chin. "Personally, I never delved. She's… she was in her thirties. Is that too young to have enough money to buy a farm?"

Faith rolled her eyes. "Yes. Unless you hit it big in some start up or you inherit from a distant relative."

"I wouldn't know," Joyce said, "I've worked all my life." Looking at Abby, she explained, "I got a little help from family to set myself up in the café. Since I live above the café, I've never had to think about buying myself a house."

"But you must be thinking it now that you're unofficially engaged," Faith said.

Joyce tilted her head from side to side. "Bradford

lives above his store. I live above my store. Maybe we can have a rooftop extension and meet each other half way."

"You already do," Faith murmured.

"I'll pretend I didn't hear that. Anyhow, Miranda Hoppers didn't appear to have money problems so I assume she had enough to maintain an independent lifestyle."

Abby sifted through her mental notes. "When she crashed the photo shoot she brought a man with her. For some reason, I assumed they were together, as in, romantically involved."

Joyce looked at Faith. "I don't remember seeing a wedding ring on her, but she did have an impressive diamond ring. Perhaps she was engaged and, now that I think about it, there was a man who used to visit her. I often saw them drive by together and I could always tell when he spent the weekend with her because she didn't come into the café."

Faith added a piece of paper next to Miranda's name. "Big question mark for martial status and a stick man for our mystery man who could turn out to be the killer." Faith swung around to face them. "I belong to the Eden Thespians and I never heard her mention a husband or a fiancé. Also, I guess I'm not as observant as Joyce. I never noticed the diamond ring."

Abby sat up. "I'd forgotten about you being an Eden Thespian. Gordon Fisher mentioned an existing rivalry between Miranda and Kitty Belmont. What do you know about it?"

"Are we really adding Kitty to the suspect list?" Faith asked.

"What sort of answer is that?" Joyce sat up. "I'd almost believe you're trying to tell us there are grounds for suspicion because maybe you overheard Kitty threatening Miranda."

"I'm not entirely comfortable talking about one of my fellow thespians. It's... it's almost like a sorority. We've more or less pledged allegiance to one another."

"It's a theater club not a marriage," Abby said. "But you're right about not suspecting anyone yet. I think it might be too early to start the mud slinging." Abby took a sip of her coffee and sighed with appreciation. "You might not want to give us details, but can you maybe give us a hint? Do you think she had motive to kill Miranda? Let me rephrase that. Do you think their rivalry justified killing her?"

Faith gave it some thought. "Miranda could be difficult. I'm not surprised she was an only child. She certainly displayed the traits." Faith shrugged. "Just saying. If we are going to point the finger of suspicion at Kitty, we'll have to assume Miranda went too far. What exactly went on at the photo shoot?"

"I got the feeling Miranda wanted to bait Kitty into overreacting. At one point, Kitty used her parasol to threaten her." Abby slumped back and closed her eyes.

"A part of me thinks we should all go home and pick up where we left off tomorrow," Faith said. "However, I get the feeling we need to go through everything now. Write down as much as we can come up with and—"

Abby sprung upright. "The photos."

"Yes," Joyce exclaimed. "I forgot about those."

Abby grabbed her phone and sent all the photos she'd taken to her laptop only to remember she didn't have a printer. "Do you want me to send copies to the office?" she asked Faith.

"That would be a good idea. I can print them and we can recreate the scene."

Abby looked at her wall. "Do you plan on camping out here tonight?"

"That's a great idea. I should go home and get a change of clothes." Faith checked the time. "It's close to dinner time for my dogs. That's usually the only time they pay attention to me. The rest of the time they're next door playing with my neighbor's dog. I'll be back in half an hour. Don't discuss anything too important."

Joyce stretched her arms over head. "I'll stay a while but I'll need to go home tonight. I have deliveries early tomorrow morning." She fidgeted with her phone. "There are too many photos to send and my phone's running low on battery. I'll run them off on my printer tomorrow and bring them in."

Abby leaned forward and stared blankly at the wall. She didn't want to think about a mantle of suspicion falling over everyone who lived in Eden.

"Assuming this is a suspicious death, what do you think Joshua will do first?" Joyce asked.

"He'll probably want to talk to everyone who knew Miranda Hoppers and try to retrace her steps before she met her end."

"Shouldn't that be her 'untimely' end?"

"Yes, of course."

"I guess I should prepare to be interrogated." Joyce crossed her legs and fell silent.

After a few minutes, Abby looked at her and laughed. "Are you running through what you'll say to Joshua or deciding what you're going to wear?"

"I feel I should take offense." After a few moments, Joyce laughed too. "Fine, I'll admit I did both. Anyhow, back to Joshua's modus operandi."

Abby sat back. "I assume motive will be a priority with him. People always have a reason for killing. Jealousy. Greed. Revenge. Anger."

"Is there such a thing as unjustified homicide?" Joyce asked. "I hope not because then we'll have to start locking our doors and hiring bodyguards."

When Joyce fell silent again, Abby couldn't help looking at her.

"What?" Joyce asked.

"You always have something to say."

"I can be pensive too." Sighing, Joyce shrugged. "It can't be a local. I know that's what I said last time, and I'm trying not to think about that. We think we know someone and then… we don't." Joyce surged to her feet. "This is going to keep me up all night. How long do you think it'll take to find out if we're dealing with a murder case?"

A knock at the door had them both stilling.

"I suddenly feel the urge to hide," Joyce said.

Doyle strutted to the door and sniffed the floor.

"Who is it Doyle?" Joyce asked.

Abby snorted. "I hope you don't expect him to answer."

The door handle turned.

Joyce gasped and grabbed hold of Abby. "Someone is trying to break into your apartment," she whispered.

They both edged toward the door.

"Shouldn't we head for the fire escape?" Joyce asked.

"Doyle is wagging his tail, but I guess I should make sure." Abby cleared her throat. "Who goes there? Friend or foe?"

"It's Markus and I'm carrying a tray of food. A little help would be appreciated."

"How do we know it's really you?" Joyce asked.

Markus grumbled.

"Yes, I suppose that sounds like Markus." Abby opened the door a crack. "And it looks like him. Complete with a scowl. Come in. This is mighty nice of you."

Markus set the tray down on the coffee table. "Don't thank me, this was Mitch's idea." When he straightened, he looked at the wall. "Is this what you girls do for fun?"

"In case you haven't heard, we were the ones who found… the victim," Joyce said. "I believe we can use our combined powers of observation to uncover the culprit."

Markus gave them both one of his rare smiles. "The victim. You mean, Miranda Hoppers."

They both gasped. Of course… he'd seen the name written on the wall. "You can't tell anyone. Swear to us you won't." Abby hitched her hands on her waist and tried to look intimidating.

"Yeah, sure. I won't tell a living soul."

"Would you mind telling us where you were this morning?" Joyce asked.

"I do mind."

Joyce hummed. "Uncooperative witness. What are you hiding?"

"My personal life," Markus said.

"I see. Does that mean you were with a certain someone?" Joyce asked. "I could ask Hannah to corroborate your whereabouts."

"Good luck with that."

"You sound sure of her silence. Are you two conspiring?"

Chuckling, Markus turned his attention back to the wall. "You're missing photos."

Abby pointed toward her laptop. "We have plenty of them but I don't have a printer."

Markus grinned. "I can help with that."

CHAPTER 5

"When I came back and found Markus sitting on the floor cross-legged and surrounded by the photos he'd helped print out, I could have sworn I'd stepped into another dimension," Faith said as she stretched and yawned.

Abby bent down to pick up Doyle's water bowl. "I had a similar experience a second ago when I strode into my sitting room and found you stretched out on my couch. What time did we eventually turn in last night?"

"Let me see…" Faith raked her fingers through her hair. "The first time we tried to shove Markus out the door, it was just after one in the morning. I think he eventually left at two. I had no idea he could talk so much."

"I guess working at the bar he gets to hear as much gossip as Joyce does at the café. Actually, his gossip is probably far superior since most people tend to loosen their tongues after a couple of drinks." Abby strode into the little galley kitchen and washed out Doyle's bowls. "Are you showering here or do you need to get home to your dogs?"

"They had a sleep over at my neighbor's house. She'll look after them. If you don't mind, I'll grab a quick shower here and then head over to the office to open up." Faith yelped. "Seven o'clock? What am I doing awake at seven in the morning?"

"Sorry, I thought you knew."

"No. Do you always get up at this uncivilized hour?"

"What can I say? I like to watch the sunrise. If I don't, I spend the day feeling I've missed out on something."

"I would never have picked you for an early bird. Doyle is still asleep."

"He's pretending. Usually, he's the one waking me up. He knows today is bath day." Abby set the bowl of water and food down and checked her phone. Nothing from Joshua. She switched on the laptop and scanned the online newspapers.

Faith yawned again. "If you don't mind, I'll linger for a bit longer."

"In that case, I'll grab a quick shower." Abby usually came up with her brightest ideas when she showered. She supposed she'd have to settle for a quick flash of inspiration…

❧

Fifteen minutes later, inspiration struck. They could use the photos to create a collage of the picnic.

Pulling on a sweater, Abby strode into the sitting room. When she heard Faith chatting, she said, "I'm glad I'm not the only one who talks to Doyle. He's a good listener."

Faith laughed. "Doyle woke up for a second and then went right back to sleep. I'm actually chatting with your mom." Faith pointed to the laptop. "She called while you were in the shower."

Abby tried to stay out of the line of vision and gestured to the wall. If her mom had seen their crime board, she'd scream for Abby to come straight back home.

"Where are you? I can't see you," her mom said.

"Hi mom." She sat next to Faith and waved.

"Faith told me you girls had a late night last night. Any news about that poor woman?"

Belatedly, Abby remembered her mom had seen Miranda on the boat.

"Abby? Do you know how she died?"

"We're still waiting to hear, mom."

"I suppose there's no point in worrying about you."

Abby couldn't tell if her mom was trying her hand at being sarcastic or if she'd come to terms with the fact her daughter was over thirty years old and could look after herself.

"You know you'll be the first to know when I hear something."

"That's what you told Mitch," her mom said.

How did she know?

"I spoke with him a short while ago," her mom said, clearly using her uncanny ability to read Abby's mind.

"How… How did you get his number?"

"You gave me the number for the pub in case of an emergency. Or have you forgotten?"

Yes, but… Why had her mom felt compelled to call Mitch?

"Joyce was no better. I actually thought she might share something with me."

Abby's voice hitched. "You called Joyce too?"

"I'm going to grab that shower now," Faith said.

Leaving Abby to face the music alone. "Just how many people in Eden are you in touch with?"

"Your mom worries about you because she wants you to be happy. I don't see anything wrong with that," Faith said as they stepped out of the pub.

"I wasn't thinking about her. Right now, there's only enough headspace to think about breakfast at Joyce's." Abby grumbled. "My mom's obsessed with living in a crime-free zone. There's no such utopia." Doyle stopped at the curb. "Come on, Doyle. There's no traffic." Abby looked up. "Oh."

"Oh," Faith echoed. "I warned you there'd be a mob after you."

They both stepped back from the curb, their eyes on

the crowd of people gathered outside the Eden Rise Gazette across the street.

"Is that normal?" Abby asked. She'd only been living in Eden for a few short weeks and while she'd been exposed to the oddities of the small town, she hadn't experienced anything to worry about, certainly nothing to send her packing.

"I've never seen this happen," Faith mused. "Do they look agitated to you?"

Abby nodded. "They look a little restless."

Doyle looked over his shoulder and, realizing they'd both stepped back, he scurried toward the pub.

"I think Doyle has the right idea. We should go back inside," Faith suggested.

Abby stopped at the door and turned. "What do you think they want?"

"Your head, of course. I told you that article would be bad news."

"Nonsense. I think they're clamoring for news about Miranda Hoppers." Abby checked her cell phone. Still no news from Joshua.

"That's just it. They don't know it was Miranda Hoppers in that body bag. And maybe that's the reason they're outside the Gazette. They've all decided they won't spend another night in the dark and now demand some answers, starting with the name of the victim."

"In that case, they should be targeting the police," Abby reasoned. Then again, the police were located in the next town… Abby stepped away from the door.

"Hey, what are you doing? Where are you going?"

"To see what they want, of course. I can't live in a state of fear." Although, what if they did want her head because of the article she'd written about the possible extinction of chocolate?

"I thought you were going to be sensible." Sighing, Faith followed her while Doyle trailed behind at a safe distance.

"Good morning, everyone." The hum of conversation came to a stop. Everyone turned to look at Abby. A woman nudged the man standing beside her. He cleared his throat.

"You're the new reporter," he said.

"I am. Hi." Abby's throat constricted slightly. They didn't look like a mob out for blood. No pitchforks in sight, Abby thought, but they did look tense.

"Is the newspaper going to run a story about what happened at the lake?" the man asked. "We've been glued to the radio all day and still no word about the identity of the victim or the cause of death."

"And that's as much as we know," Abby said as Faith stepped up and came to stand beside her.

"Rubbish. We saw you talking to the detective," the man said. Everyone around him agreed with nods.

"And you can imagine how that conversation went," Abby said. "I've been warned to wait until the next of kin have been informed. And that's as much as I am allowed to say."

The man straightened. "That's not good enough."

"I agree, but unfortunately that's the way things

stand. The police have to do their job and we have to think of the relatives."

The man didn't look convinced. "We have kids." He put his arm around the woman.

Faith stepped forward. "How would you like it if everyone else found out a family member had died before you did?"

"Our hearts go out to them," the man said. "But why isn't anyone saying anything? We have a right to know."

"And you will be informed as soon as we get the go-ahead from the police," Abby assured him. She thought she heard someone say they should all go to Joyce's café because she was bound to know more. Abby wished them all good luck. When the crowd dispersed, she felt her shoulders ease down a notch. "I guess that was touch and go."

"Yeah," Faith agreed. "I've never seen them like this."

And now they were all headed to Joyce's. "I suppose we could go back to the pub for breakfast."

"Where's your spirit of adventure?" Faith grabbed hold of Abby's arm and tugged her along.

"Hey, a moment ago you were all for hiding at the pub."

"That was then, this is now." Faith tugged her again. "I'm curious to see how this unfolds."

"Come on, Doyle. No lagging behind. We're in this together."

Faith waved at a passerby. "Considering what just

happened, after we've had breakfast, I think it might be a good idea to work from your place."

"Are you referring to actual work or to sticking our noses where they don't belong?" Abby asked.

Faith harrumphed. "Whatever happened to investigative reporting?"

Abby raised her hands to the heavens. "I'm not a crime reporter. I'm a lifestyle and leisure reporter."

"I've never heard your whiny tone. I'm surprised Doyle didn't join in with a howl. Is it unusual or something I should expect on a regular basis?"

"It was nothing but an instinctive outburst. Sorry," Abby offered.

When they reached Joyce's Café, they saw everyone who'd stood outside the Gazette had taken up most of the tables.

Abby looked up and down the street. "There should be an alternative to Joyce's."

"We could go to the bakery but then Joyce will be annoyed with us. Also, they don't serve coffee." Faith gave her a gentle push. "Relax. The mob already had a go at you."

"It's so comforting to have you as my ally." They strode into the café and immediately drew everyone's attention. "I get the feeling they disapprove of us being here, taking time out for breakfast."

"You set the bar, Abby. What do you expect?"

Abby's eyebrows rose. "What do you mean?"

"You solved Dermot's case. Everyone expect

answers from you. They want you to step up to the plate."

"Good morning," Joyce greeted them. "Table for two?" She looked down at Doyle and, as promised, pretended he wasn't there. As far as she was concerned, if Parisians allowed dogs into their restaurants and cafés, then so would she.

"Thank you." Abby raised her voice so everyone could hear her. "We're here for breakfast."

"Yes, of course. This way please." Joyce led them to a table by the window. "I see you've drawn some attention." Joyce tapped her pen against her chin. "I wonder what that's about?"

"I'm sure you know." Abby picked up the extensive menu. "I'll have the 'Extraordinary Break Your Fast Platter' and a Midnight Express without the swagger." Too early for a shot of brandy in her coffee, Abby thought, even though the circumstances called for it.

"You think you can fit that size breakfast into you?" Faith read the description. "Sausages, tomatoes, mushrooms, sunny side up eggs, bacon, hash browns, baked beans followed by blueberry pancakes."

She'd probably struggle. "Leave the baked beans out, please. I'll take my time with the rest and pace myself." While they waited, she drew out her cell phone and did a quick search online. "Miranda had the usual social presence online posting photos of herself onstage."

"Let me see." Faith leaned in. "Oh, yes. That's from

our production of Cat on a Hot Tin Roof. She started out as Kitty's understudy."

"Let me guess, she played the leading role because something happened to Kitty?"

Faith's eyebrows drew down. "Kitty sprung a leak and her house flooded."

"Really?" Abby lowered her voice to a whisper. "Did anyone suspect Miranda of tampering with the pipes?"

Faith didn't answer. Instead, she looked at Abby without blinking.

"Do you need me to click my fingers?" Abby asked.

"I can't believe it didn't occur to me. Their altercations were almost like taking little bites out of each other and one never knew who'd instigated the arguments. They'd erupt, flare up, explode and then they'd each step away and act as if nothing had happened." Faith took a long sip of water. "Now that I think about it, they were always well-timed. I'd even go so far as to say they were staged. Only one or two people ever witnessed them and never from close up so it was hard to even determine what had been said."

Very smart, Abby thought. If she wanted to create friction, she imagined she'd do it subtly. A little bit at a time.

"Did Kitty ever mention anything about what Miranda had said or done?" Abby asked.

Faith shook her head. "Let me think… If she did, it would have been a passing remark. You know the type you have to put two and two together."

Yes, Abby knew exactly what she meant. When Kitty had seen Miranda arriving, she'd said…

"How dare Miranda show up. That's what Kitty said the day of the picnic photo shoot."

"Yes, that sounds about right. You wouldn't have known what to make of it." Faith leaned in and whispered. "What did you make of it?"

An open-ended remark such as that one would have been open to interpretation and all sorts of wild speculation. "I asked Gordon if there was some sort of rivalry between them." Abby shrugged. "After that, I didn't give it much thought. In fact, Doyle and I moved away and explored the area."

"You'd make a dreadful gossip columnist. Dear Abby, in case you didn't notice this, I'll tell you…"

Abby rolled her eyes and resumed her search online. "I'm hoping to find some sort of mention of her partner. Maybe even an engagement announcement." She scrolled through Miranda's social media page. "She liked posting photos of herself in poses. I'm guessing these are clothes from the wardrobe department." She showed Faith the pictures.

"Yes." Faith chuckled. "Isn't that odd. Kitty wore most of those gowns for her leading roles. I think Miranda might have been trying them on for size." Faith clicked her fingers. "That makes sense. I remember Kitty making a passing remark once and I thought she'd been talking to herself."

"What did she say?"

"She complained about the perfume on her dress.

She's sensitive to smell and had to have the dress cleaned."

"I get the feeling Miranda enjoyed playing mind games." And she targeted Kitty Belmont because Kitty got all the leading roles.

Joyce approached their table and set down a couple of plates. "French Toast for Faith and the *Extraordinary Break Your Fast* for you. Enjoy."

"What's with the raised eyebrow look?" Abby asked. "Are you questioning my choice of breakfast? It's in your menu."

"Actually, no woman has ever ordered that at my café. It's always been a favorite with men. It's just an observation. Are you, by any chance, stress eating?"

"No." Abby looked around the café. People had stopped openly staring at her but they continued glancing her way.

"They're going to give me indigestion," Abby complained.

"Would you like me to tell them to stop looking at you?" Joyce asked.

"Would you be so kind?"

"Of course."

Abby waited for Joyce to move on before saying, "I think Joyce wields more power in this town than is safe."

Faith agreed with a nod. "It's the suffer no fools way of looking she has. I've actually stood in front of the mirror trying to mimic it."

"Show me."

"Nope. I look like a caricature. Nothing but a wannabe Joyce. She's one of a kind."

Abby patted Faith's hand. "You are unique and you excel at bossing me around."

"Thank you. Now, eat up."

It took three cups of coffee to wash down her super sized breakfast and when she finished, she had to discreetly loosen her belt.

"Did you eat all that because you felt everyone watching you or because you were really hungry?" Faith asked.

"The truth? A little of both. I kept thinking what people here would say. That new reporter is slow to take action but she sure can pack it in. It'd be cheaper to buy her a dress than to invite her over for dinner." Abby laughed.

She resumed her search online and within a few minutes exclaimed, "I found something. Miranda's engagement announcement." Abby cleared her throat. "Miranda Hoppers and William Matthews have set the date. The happy couple will honeymoon in the Maldives. That's all it says. This is dated three months ago."

"She never mentioned anything to us," Faith mused. "You'd think she'd say something."

"Joyce said she noticed her ring, but you didn't."

Faith tilted her head in thought. "I'm sure I did notice and I think it might have been a case of oh, she's wearing a ring and then being distracted by something else."

"The Maldives. That's expensive," Abby mused.

Faith finished her coffee and looked around for Joyce. "I wouldn't mind another one, thank you."

As Joyce cleared the table, she said, "I couldn't help noticing you're on the phone. Are you researching?"

"Yes, you can tell everyone I'm on the case... in case there is a case."

Joyce gave her one of her enigmatic smiles. "I see. You're afraid they'll get on your case because you're not on the case?"

"Yes."

"In that case, I'll leave you to it."

"Is there any mention of what this William Matthews character does for a living?" Faith asked.

Abby continued trawling for information. "Merchant banker. I don't see any mention of which bank he works for and there are no details about how they met. I find that odd. Usually, there's a cute back-story. You know, they met while on vacation or they were introduced."

Faith shifted in her seat. "I like blind-date stories. When I was at school, a bunch of us went to a lot of trouble to get these two friends together. We'd noticed sparks but they were stuck in the denial stage so we planned a trip to the city and made sure they got on the bus, then we skipped out on them. Luckily they decided to make the best of it and spent a weekend together following the schedule we'd organized. They went to the theater, the movies and galleries. We even booked restaurants for them. It's been five years and they're still together." Faith took a sip of her coffee. "Your mouth is gaping open and you're staring at me."

"I... I've never known anyone to do that for a friend."

Faith grinned. "You need to get some quality friends."

"More coffee?" Joyce offered as she strode by their table.

"Y-yes, please." Abby's eyes zeroed in on the person who'd just walked into the café. Detective Joshua Ryan placed his order at the counter. When he turned, he spotted Abby.

Their eyes locked.

Abby gave him a lifted eyebrow look.

He returned the eyebrow lift.

Abby tilted her head and narrowed her brows.

One by one, everyone in the café turned to look at him.

"I feel the pressure is off me now," Abby murmured. "That's something, but... He owes me." After all, she had been instrumental in finding Dermot's killer.

With his coffee in hand, he took a step toward the door only to stop.

"I swear if he doesn't give us an update, I will hunt him down."

"And do what to him?" Faith asked.

"I'll... I'll torture him with a detailed description of an English chintz filled sitting room."

Joshua took a sip of his coffee, headed toward their table and, without asking, he drew out a chair.

"You're here to give us an update," Abby stated.

He gave her a small nod. "Bee sting."

"What about it?"

"Miranda died from a bee sting."

CHAPTER 6

A bee sting!

"She had an allergic reaction to it," Joshua explained.

Abby remembered to blink. A dozen questions pushed and shoved around her mind and tried to make their way out of her mouth. She grabbed her cell phone and looked up bee stings.

"Death can come from heart failure," she read. "An allergic reaction occurs when the body's defense system overreacts, causing breathing difficulties, low blood pressure and a swelling of the face, tongue, mouth and lips so that the airways become obstructed." Abby looked up and found Joyce staring at her, eyes unblinking. They both nodded as if suddenly making sense of Miranda's bloated face. Abby frowned. "How long does it take to die from a bee sting?"

Joshua twirled his coffee cup around in his hands. "Depends. There was a recent case of a man in his late forties who died ten days after being stung, but he was over 6ft tall and weighed 240 pounds. Miranda's slim body and medium height might have worked against her. A woman in England was in a coma for two years before she died. In another recent case, a man was stung on the neck and died in front of his wife before the ambulance could get to him."

"Anaphylactic shock," Faith mused. "People with allergies to bee stings are supposed to carry an emergency pack of adrenaline-filled syringes to counter the effects."

"Maybe Miranda didn't know she had an allergy," Abby said.

Joshua shook his head. "She knew about it. In fact, she wore a bracelet with a red cross on it clearly stating her allergy."

"Did she have a bag with her on the boat?" Abby didn't remember seeing one.

"No."

That's odd, Abby thought. If she knew she had an allergy, she would take precautions and carry an adrenaline shot everywhere she went. "So, are you saying this is a death by natural causes?"

Joshua didn't answer straight away. He finished his coffee and when Joyce offered him another one, he nodded. "Yes, for the time being," he finally said under his breath.

Abby slumped back on her chair. "Have the next of kin been notified?"

"She didn't have any parents. We found a cousin and her husband. He's making the funeral arrangements."

"Wait, did you say husband?" Abby hadn't found any mention of a husband. When had she married William Matthews?

"Yes. He's a merchant banker."

"William Matthews?"

"You must be the only person in town who knows his name," Joshua remarked. "I spoke with Miranda's neighbors and none of them ever met him."

"I've been trawling the internet looking for information about Miranda," she admitted. "There was mention of an engagement but nothing about a marriage."

Joshua stirred some sugar into his coffee. "According to him, they'd set a date for twelve month's time but Miranda then suggested they elope. Apparently they were arguing about all the details," Joshua shrugged. "Venue, flowers, cakes, number of guests. It all got a bit too much so they opted for an easy solution."

"How did you find out about him?"

"We have easy access to the births and deaths registry as well as the marriages registry."

He'd sat on that information for a whole day...

Abby was about to tell him off for not sharing when his phone rang. Excusing himself, he left.

A bee sting, Abby mouthed. "Just as well I didn't run that story about the extinction of bees. It would have been too macabre."

After breakfast, they finally made their way to the Gazette. Abby and Faith worked in silence while Doyle used the opportunity to curl up on his doggie bed to enjoy a morning nap.

A few locals dropped by to confirm what they'd heard. No one made any further comments. As far as everyone was concerned, Miranda Hoppers had run into some serious bad luck.

Abby got busy writing a brief summary of events and a death announcement but hit a wall when she tried to find a positive spin for the article. With such a somber and delicate subject, she had to tread with care and not put people off the lake. She knew it would be a while before the incident receded into a distant memory, but the lake wouldn't go away. Somehow, she had to find a way to cleanse it. Maybe not straight away...

She stretched her arms over her head and yawned. "There's a downside to having such a hearty breakfast. It makes me sleepy. I want to curl up with Doyle." She looked around the office. "Hey, why don't we have a couch?"

Faith laughed. "Why? Because you'd probably spend the day curled up on it. I did an office management course online. Efficiency and productivity drops after lunch. People become sluggish."

Only on a slow news day, Abby thought. "Businesses and stores in some European countries close their doors in the early afternoon for siesta time. It makes sense."

Faith agreed. "That's one civilized practice I wish would be adopted by everyone. If only it still meant finishing work at five, but I'm guessing you have to work until later."

"Yeah, there's always a catch." Abby looked out the window and toward the pub. "At least I don't have far to go to hit the hay."

"Are you going to make the pub your permanent home?" Faith asked.

"I don't see why not. The apartment is roomy and comfortable. The service is excellent. Doyle gets the royal treatment and the staff are super friendly."

"It sounds like an ideal bachelor existence. Surely you want more," Faith remarked.

"Maybe." Abby leaned back in her office chair and swung from side to side. She still hadn't shared the woeful experience she'd had with her ex and she preferred to keep it that way.

"What's wrong? Why are you frowning?"

"Am I?" Abby ran her finger across her forehead.

"There's a deep wedge between your eyebrows."

Swinging around, Abby sat up. "Did Joshua sound odd when he said Miranda had died of a bee sting?"

Faith shrugged. "I didn't notice. He's always so hard to read."

"Yes, Sebastian said he did the inscrutable look really well." After his grandfather's funeral, the new Eden Rise Gazette owner had returned to the city but had phoned at least once a week for updates. He'd actually offered her the keys to his grandfather's cottage in town, but Abby had felt odd about accepting. She knew there were no strings attached, but it was still too soon after discovering a body there... Also, for the time being at least, she wanted to stay on at the pub. Abby thought it would give her an advantage to be so close to the hive of activity and gossip.

Abby surged to her feet. "Did Joshua actually say Miranda had died of natural causes?"

"Let me think." Faith tapped a pen on her desk. "He said, for now. No, wait... For the time being, that's what he said."

Meaning what?

Faith lowered her voice. "There's just cause for suspicion and he's going to hold his cards close to his chest and try to flush out the bee responsible for stinging Miranda."

Abby shook her head. "Bees actually die after stinging someone or something."

"Really? That's like having a booby-trapped revolver. You shoot someone and the revolver then explodes in your face."

Abby strode to the window. "Also, while I'm sure everyone in the café heard him, he left it up to us to spread the word. Maybe you're right. He's suspicious and wants the perpetrator to make a false move." If someone died from a bee sting, why would Joshua be suspicious?

"Then again, you might be reading too much into it," Faith suggested.

"You're right."

Bee sting…

Something didn't smell right about that.

Faith sat opposite Abby at what had become their regular table at the pub, right by the windows with a view of the mountains.

"I think Joyce might have been onto something when she said you were stress eating."

"It's lunch time," Abby murmured. "Everyone stops for lunch."

"Yes, but… you've been studying the menu for longer than you usually do. That means you're going to order something other than a burger."

Abby bobbed her head from side to side. "I might want to try something new. Variety is the spice of life and I'm trying to avoid becoming predictable and falling into a rut."

Doyle thumped his tail against her foot.

"I think Doyle agrees with me."

"Okay. For a moment there I thought you might have been lost in thought and might be pursuing the possibility that there's more to Miranda's death."

Abby picked up a breadstick and wagged it at Faith. "That would be asking for trouble."

Faith ignored her and continued, "Either that or

85

you're answering the call of the inner reporter. You've been quiet because you're entertaining a barrage of thoughts and you can sniff a scoop in the making."

Admittedly, Abby had been playing around with a few thoughts but they refused to take full shape or make sense.

"Ready to order?" Mitch asked.

The co-owner of the Gloriana flipped open his order book and tapped his pen against it. His bright blue eyes smiled back at her. Since meeting him, Abby hadn't seen any other look on Mitch Faydon, which boded well for all the customers coming to the pub. The same couldn't be said for his brother Markus who rather enjoyed scowling. Abby knew there was a third brother, but she hadn't met him yet because he was still away on a long vacation.

Abby sat back and gave Mitch a head to toe sweep. "Aren't you going to ask?"

"If I do, will you give me a straight answer?"

Abby grinned. "Try me."

"Is the bee sting story a cover up?" Mitch asked.

Abby looked at Faith. "See, it's not just me."

Faith laughed. "Are you actually admitting you've been thinking about it?"

Mitch looked around and lowered his voice. "What's going on?"

Abby gestured for him to pull up a chair. "When Joshua told us about the medical examiner's findings—"

"We call them coroners here," Mitch said.

"M.E. Coroner. Same thing. They cut bodies up.

Anyhow, Joshua's general tone suggested he might not be convinced it was a death by natural causes."

"So the bee didn't do it?" Mitch asked.

"I believe there are suspicious circumstances." Abby tapped her finger on the table. "Mark my word, the truth is out there."

Mitch laughed. "I thought you were strictly a lifestyle reporter. What's come over you?"

"It might be a case of wanting to check my facts. After all, it's my by-line. My name is my reputation and once I print the report on the picnic incident, that'll be it." At the same time, she didn't want to be responsible for causing civil unrest in the community. The locals had already been uneasy about the lack of information. What would happen if she suggested Miranda's death needed to be investigated further?

"Forget I said anything." Abby picked up the menu again. "I need to have something nourishing and filling but not too filling. What would you recommend?"

"Hannah can whip you up a quinoa and wild rice salad," Mitch suggested.

"That sounds… healthy."

"You can always have a steak with the lot."

Abby patted her stomach. "I pigged out at breakfast so I need to take it down a notch for lunch."

"Quinoa and rice salad it is then." He turned to Faith. "The usual for you?"

"Yes, please."

Abby leaned in. "What's that?"

Faith grinned. "A burger with the lot, of course."

Abby threw her head back and groaned. "You're going to eat that in front of me?"

"Moderation is the key to a full and healthy life," Faith declared.

"Well, as the saying goes, breakfast like a king, lunch like a prince and dine like a pauper." Abby looked over her shoulder but Mitch had already disappeared. "Darn it. I'm sure princes don't eat quinoa and rice salad for lunch."

Distracting herself with another breadstick, she wondered if she should have a test for bee stings. "How does one know?"

"Do you expect an answer or are you talking to yourself?" Faith asked.

"Do you know if you're allergic to bee stings?"

Faith shook her head. "I have no idea."

"I guess it wouldn't hurt to know."

"I wouldn't worry too much about the humble bee," Faith said. "We have more deadly critters than any other country in the world."

Abby laughed. "You say that with so much pride, but I guess you're right. I read about them on my flight over. Just as well I'm not really into swimming. The beaches here are too crowded for my liking. There's stinging stonefish..."

Faith grinned. "Yeah, the pain of a sting from one of those can be lethal. It produces such mind-blowing agony that the body goes into shock and the person dies. Then there's the pretty blue-ringed octopus. They're quite small but they have one of the most toxic venoms on the planet and a bite causes paralysis within minutes. That leads to respiratory issues and then heart failure. I'm sure you'll find more if you research it."

Doing a search on her cell phone, Abby found an article listing seventy-two deadly creatures. They discussed each one with Faith providing a few stories about her close encounters with spiders.

"Redback spiders are everywhere. They're only small but the red blotch on their backs is quite distinctive. You just have to be careful in the garden and sheds. And they're not exclusive to the countryside." Faith shook her head. "I once visited a cousin who'd moved to the city to study. There I was, waiting to cross a street, when I looked down and saw a redback waiting right alongside me."

"I find that hard to believe."

"And yet it happened."

"Okay. This is interesting." Abby read through to the end of the article and gasped. "More deaths are caused by the European honey bee. This species doesn't have a particularly potent venom, but the allergic reaction suffered by 1-2 per cent of the population coupled with the high incidence of bee stings make them second to snakes as the most deadly venomous animal in Australia."

They both looked out the window.

"They're out there," Abby whispered. "I guess there's no harm in making sure we're not allergic."

Faith nodded. "I'll book us an appointment."

Mitch approached and set their plates down.

Abby studied her wild rice salad. "This actually looks rather appetizing and colorful." Mixed in with the wild rice, she could see red and green bell peppers, bright orange pumpkin, hard-boiled egg with happy looking yellow-orange yolks, spinach leaves and what looked like feta cheese. "Are these poppy seeds?"

"Black chia seeds and the white ones are the quinoa," Mitch said. "It's a super food. Eat up, it's good for you."

Faith took a bite of her burger and gave a heavenly sigh.

Spooning a mouthful of her salad, Abby smiled. "Like the man said, it's good for me."

Mitch strode off saying, "But not as good as a burger."

Half an hour later, Abby couldn't believe how full she felt. "I think I read something about chia seeds giving you a feeling of fullness. Maybe I should sprinkle some on all my meals."

Faith chortled. "It's not as if you have weight issues."

"Not yet," Abby murmured. "I've been told it sneaks up on you."

"So what's on for the rest of the day?"

"I need to have my picnic clothes dry cleaned before they go back to the wardrobe department. Also, I think it would help if we walk around a bit and try to pick up on the general vibe. People must be talking. Who knows what we'll hear…"

"There's a slight tear on the blouse. Are you able to fix it?" Abby asked.

Jacinta Smith, the owner of Pristine Dry Cleaners, hummed as she examined the delicate fabric. "I couldn't get anyone to cover for me so I didn't get to go to the picnic but I heard there was quite a commotion." Jacinta looked up and pushed her glasses back. "Yes, this shouldn't be a problem. We have several items requiring mending."

Abby felt slightly less guilty. She remembered hearing the tear when she'd bent down to free her shoe. "Who else damaged their clothes?"

"Kitty Belmont lost a button on her skirt," Jacinta said. "That might be hard to replace. It was a mother of pearl button. They don't make them like they used to." She handed Abby a receipt. "It'll be ready in two days."

"Thank you." As they strode away, Abby turned to Faith. "I remember seeing Kitty fiddling with her skirt. Doyle and I had been strolling around and..." Abby tapped her chin. "And then we saw the rowboat." Abby stopped. "Hang on. I need to get this right. My mind is swimming with information. I started taking photos when we arrived. Then Doyle and I went for a walk. We encountered Kitty and Gordon. He waved me over and offered me a glass of champagne. That's when I saw Kitty adjusting her skirt." And somewhere in-between she'd noticed the boat out in the middle of the lake. At the time, she hadn't seen anyone on it.

"What?"

"I'm trying to remember something about the rowboat I saw. I think that's when I noticed it out in the middle of the lake." Had the current pushed it toward the shore? Was there a current on the lake? There had to be...

She looked down at Doyle and remembered she had booked him in for his bath. Laughing to herself, she imagined Doyle rolling his eyes at her and huffing. Of all the things to remember...

"I'd like to know what Kitty did to lose the button on her skirt." Did she bend over to maybe haul something heavy? "We'll have to go to the lake and have a look around. Let's swing by the Gazette and grab the camera."

"What if the police taped off the area?" Faith asked. "They tend to do that. At least, they do on the crime shows I've watched."

"We'll tackle that hurdle when we get to it."

CHAPTER 7

"That's the fourth person we've heard talking about bees," Faith said as they turned a corner and headed back to the Gazette.

"It might be a good idea to run an article about the possible extinction of bees after all."

Faith's eyebrows shot up. "You think people will find that comforting?"

"I guess not," Abby said. "Without bees, we'd have no cross-pollination. They're such productive little creatures, I hate to see them being put under such a negative spotlight."

When Abby strode past the Gazette, Faith tugged her arm. "I thought we were going back to grab the camera."

Abby pressed her finger to her lips and then mouthed the word 'bath'. "Oh, I need to pop in next door." She pointed toward the vet's office. "I shouldn't be long." Abby got as far as the front door when Doyle pulled back on his leash.

Faith laughed. "He's so smart."

"It's not that he doesn't enjoy being clean. A couple of weeks ago, Katherine used a new shampoo and Doyle didn't like the perfume. He spent an hour rolling around the rug. He'd then stop and smell himself and go right back to rolling around." Abby bent down and picked him up. "Katherine likes to pamper you, Doyle. Do you want me to hurt her feelings and tell her to use a more manly shampoo?" When Doyle quivered Abby hugged him against her. "You're such a baby. Anyone would think you're afraid... or cold..." Abby looked up and frowned. "Hey, wait a minute."

"What?"

Abby looked at the trees and then up at the sky. "It's the time of year. Isn't it too cold for bees?"

Faith shrugged. "I don't know. Is it?"

It had to be. Otherwise, why would the idea come to her? Did bees hibernate? No, she didn't think so. But they probably huddled up to keep warm. She must have picked up the tidbit somewhere, probably the same place where one acquired all the other useless information that filled up the cavities of the mind.

"I knew there was something odd about the bee sting story. There has to be." Striding into the vet's, Abby asked to speak with Pete Cummings, the vet. "Oh, and Katherine. Don't take this the wrong way, but could you maybe use a shampoo that doesn't smell so pretty?"

"Detective Inspector Joshua Ryan, please." Abby tucked her hair back and tried to ignore Faith. She could only take so many eye rolls. "My name? Hermione Granger."

The receptionist sighed. "Are you sure about that? Didn't you call five minutes ago claiming to be Angie Dickinson?"

Why wouldn't Joshua talk to her? Abby had tried his direct line. She'd left a message. Okay, she'd left several messages. She'd also asked Faith to call on her behalf, and then she'd decided to pretend to be someone else.

"Would you like to leave a message?" the receptionist asked.

"Tell him I know about the bees."

"Hermione Granger knows about the bees," the receptionist said.

Abby sighed. "It's actually Abby Maguire."

"Are you sure about that?"

"It's been me all along." Abby heard chatter in the background and could have sworn someone snickered. "Actually, is Detective Inspector Quentin McNamara available?"

"Yes, of course. I'll put you through."

Really? Abby did a victory dance on the spot. She'd met Quentin McNamara for the first time at the picnic. He'd come across as the quiet type. Observant. Vigilant. Yet somehow unsuited to his job. He actually looked out of place in this alpine town. Abby didn't want to stereotype him but his blond hair and suntanned skin, broad shoulders and narrow hips made her think he'd be more suited working as a lifesaver at Bondi beach.

"Abby Maguire. What can I do for you?" he asked.

"Hello, detective. I have some questions and I was rather hoping to bounce them off Joshua, but he hasn't returned my calls." There, she'd said it.

"I'll be happy to pass along any pertinent information or answer questions. What's on your mind?"

"Bees. It's too cold for them. You tell Detective Ryan I'm onto him. Have a nice day."

Abby swung toward Faith who sat at her desk trying to hide her smile. "Can you believe Joshua? Why do you think he's not taking my calls? It's not as if I've made a nuisance of myself. I thought I'd earned his respect."

"What makes you think you haven't?"

Abby lifted her hands and shoulders. "Who knows? Maybe because he doesn't want to talk to me."

"He might be busy."

Either that or he was on the trail of something and he didn't want to share the information with her in case she decided to do her own investigating and stepped on his toes. "Come on. We have more important business to take care of. The next issue doesn't go out until the end of the week and we have to have something solid to include in it."

"Where are we going?" Faith asked.

"To the lake. Remember to grab the camera. We'll have a look around and then come back. Doyle's pampering should be done by then."

"I told you. The area has been sealed off. If we disturb the crime scene tape, Joshua will know to point the finger straight at you," Faith said.

They both sat in the car staring at the now empty picnic site. The crime scene tape had been wound around several trees, blocking off the path leading back to the private cove in the lake.

"It doesn't matter. We can still walk around the perimeter and see if we can find Kitty's button. She dropped it somewhere." And it would be a bad news day for Kitty if they found her button anywhere near the trail leading to the boat. "Let's try and be methodical about it."

"Are you suggesting we start at one end and work our way to the other?"

Abby nodded. "Side by side. It's how the police do it when they're trawling for evidence. Yes, I've seen them do it on TV."

"What makes you think we'll find something? I'm sure the police have already trawled through the area."

"They didn't know about the button." Every now and then, Abby glanced up toward the lake. The water lapped gently against the shore. She supposed the light breeze had something to do with that. All the boats had been tethered to the jetty. She couldn't help wondering if the one Miranda had been on was among them.

"What now?" Faith asked when they finished scouring the area.

Abby glanced over at the crime scene tape. "That's like waving a red flag." She couldn't see anyone around and she couldn't see the harm in walking along a path that had been trodden by dozens of people. Then again, she didn't want to be personally responsible for disturbing evidence. There had to be a reason why the police had made the area out of bounds.

She strode over to the shore. "I think we could wade our way around the overhanging bushes and over to the little cove. I'm guessing if we stick close to the shore it won't even be knee deep."

Faith gave a brisk shake of her head. "It's too soon for me, thanks. We spent our lunchtime talking about deadly critters. Reason tells me I have nothing to worry about, but fear doesn't listen to reason."

Abby had to agree. Personally, she didn't feel that keen to set foot in the water either. "There is an alternative."

"I'm listening," Faith said, her tone wary.

"We could get on a boat and row our way there."

"We could but it's getting late. I'd say we only have about fifteen minutes before the sun disappears behind those trees. I vote for coming back tomorrow."

~

"I'm not cut out for a life of adventure," Faith apologized.

"Does that mean you won't come with me to the lake tomorrow?" Abby asked, her attention fixed on the road.

"How about I sleep on it and let you know. I wouldn't want to hinder your investigation."

"It's a fact finding mission, Faith. My curiosity's been piqued." Pete Cummings had given her some basic information about bees, confirming her suspicions. When temperatures dropped into the 50s, honeybees headed to the hive and formed a winter cluster. While it wasn't the middle of winter, it still remained cool. Now, more than ever, she needed to get answers, mostly from Joshua.

Abby pulled up outside the pub just as Joyce was crossing the street.

"I brought the photos I took," Joyce said. "What are we getting up to tonight?"

"We're knuckling down and piecing together the scene of the crime," Abby said. "I'm over the initial shock of seeing Miranda dead and now that I see there are questions needing answers, I have to find those answers. I don't care what Joshua said. There is something odd about this death. But first, I have to get Doyle. You two go ahead and get started. I won't be long."

As Abby crossed the street, she thought she caught sight of Joshua driving by. "I have a bone to pick with you," she said under her breath.

At the vet's, she went through to the back room where Katherine and her assistant carried out the pet grooming side of the business. She was just finishing up with Doyle who appeared to look indifferent at Abby's appearance.

Regardless, Abby gave him a scratch under the chin. "You smell nice... in a manly way."

"I used a shampoo with a musky scent," Katherine said. "He doesn't seem to mind it. I also did a bit of clipping."

"I can see that. He looks very handsome."

Katherine hummed under her breath. "I heard you talking to Pete about bees earlier. Have there been any new developments?"

"No, not really. I was just being curious. I seem to be forever on my cell phone researching and I wanted to cut corners and ask a professional." Abby didn't want to be responsible for putting the locals on edge or feeding the rumor mills with misleading information.

"The detective came by earlier. He too wanted to know about bees and their habits."

Really? "After I spoke with Pete or before?"

"After."

As it turned out, Joshua had come by after Abby had left a message for him saying she knew about the bees. "I now have a huge bone to pick with him," she grumbled under her breath as she made her way back to the pub.

Noticing Doyle had a light sprint to his step, Abby smiled. "I guess you don't mind the musky scent."

Looking up at her, he gave her one of his doggy grins. "Now I'm thinking you didn't like the idea of being left behind. I promise to make it up to you tomorrow."

Distracted by her conversation with Doyle, she strode into the pub and didn't notice Joshua sitting at the bar, and if Mitch hadn't called out to her, she would have missed him altogether.

"The girls ordered some tea and cookies. Do me a favor and take the tray up," Mitch said.

"My pleasure," Abby said and gave Joshua a nonchalant nod.

Joshua took the tray and followed behind as she strode up the stairs. "I guess I'm in your bad books."

Abby didn't want to appear to be too eager to mend fences so she counted to ten before answering. "We seem to be headed in the same direction." Looking over her shoulder she saw him smile.

"I hear you've been working the case," he said.

After a measured pause, she nodded. "The police have been short on details so we thought we'd combine our talents to see what we can come up with. Some of us believe there might be more to Miranda's death than meets the eye. Some of us, and I'm not naming names, also believe you are withholding vital information."

"It's part of my job description." He chuckled. "By the way, I got your message today." Joshua opened the door for her and, balancing the tray, stepped back.

Doyle trotted inside and made the rounds of the apartment before settling down on his doggie bed to watch Joyce and Faith who were both busy adding more photos to the ones already on the wall.

"Here she is," Faith said. "Oh, and she's not alone. Hello detective."

"I see you've all been busy." Setting the tray down on the coffee table, he studied the collage. "When did you take these photos?"

No one answered.

He frowned and pointed at a piece of paper with Kitty's name on it. "Missing button?"

"Yes. Did the police happen to find a mother of pearl button?" Abby asked.

Joshua crossed his arms. "No."

"Did they actually search the area for evidence?"

He smiled. "What you're really asking is if I classified this incident as a murder case from the start."

"In a roundabout way. Yes." Abby sighed. "In theory, bees don't wander away from their hive when it's cold, but there is a chance that one stray bee did."

"An outlier bee?" To his credit, he didn't laugh, but his eyes glittered with amusement.

"Yes," Abby said. "It would be hard to prove one way or the other." Unless… someone deliberately introduced the bee… Abby gasped.

"What?" they all asked.

"Give me a minute." She didn't want to blurt out something that would sound ludicrous so she ran the idea through her mind first. "If I wanted to kill someone and leave no trace of evidence leading straight to me…"

Abby brushed her finger along her chin. "I would try to find the person's Achilles' heel."

"Now you're thinking like a killer," Joyce said. "Someone close to Miranda could have known about her allergy to bees."

Abby turned to Faith. "Did you? After all, you belonged to the same theater group so you liaised with her regularly."

Faith's cheeks colored slightly. "I didn't notice the engagement ring and I didn't notice the first-aid bracelet. Does that make me self-absorbed?"

"You and the vast majority of the population," Abby offered. "I constantly need to have things pointed out to me or explained."

Joyce nodded. "Yes, I still remember how puzzled you looked when you saw my menu for the first time."

"Your extraordinary menu." Abby laughed. "You should put it in a time capsule for future generations to find and puzzle over."

Joshua cleared his throat. "Tell me about the button."

Abby began telling him about it when she remembered she had a bone to pick with him. "Hey. Give and take."

He appeared to think about it. Nodding, he sat down. "I had my suspicions from the start. Miranda didn't look like the type to go out on the lake by herself." He shrugged. "Call me chauvinistic, I just couldn't imagine her rowing. So it got me thinking. Why was she alone on the boat?"

They all waited for an explanation, but Joshua didn't provide one. Instead, he looked at Abby. "Any thoughts?"

"She might have had an argument with her fiancé… I mean, her husband." Abby turned to the wall. "I haven't been able to spot him in any of the photos. Maybe she was angry with him for not going to the picnic." Abby looked at the photos again. "Where did she set up her picnic?"

"At the other end of the grounds, diagonally opposite Kitty Belmont," Joshua pointed. "About the button…"

"Hang on. Regardless of how the bee got to Miranda, why didn't anyone hear her? She must have panicked and screamed." Abby knew that if a bee came within buzzing distance of her, she'd scream. Well, she would now that the bee had become public enemy number one.

Joshua shook his head. "She had a severe reaction to the sting. According to the coroner, her airways would have been affected immediately. Now, are you going to tell me about the button?"

"I was going to all along, but you made it difficult." Abby sat down and helped herself to a cookie. "When I tried to get to the boat, my shoe got stuck. I bent down to rescue it and tore my blouse. What if Kitty exerted herself and popped a button on her skirt? Yes, Miranda had a slim frame but it would still take some effort to… I don't know, haul her onto the boat?"

"Or she might have had too much lunch," Joshua reasoned only to shake his head. "Forget I said that."

Abby silently agreed. Miranda had died well before lunch.

"Have you questioned Kitty?" Abby hadn't seen Kitty around town, but it had only been a day since the picnic.

"I'm talking to everyone associated with Miranda." He looked at Joyce and Faith.

"You can't possibly think I had anything to do with it," Joyce said. "I run a business and can't afford to alienate my customers. Why would I go around killing them?"

"What time did you arrive at the lake?" Abby asked.

"Abby! You don't seriously think I had anything to do with Miranda's unfortunate end?"

"No, but since we're in the presence of an officer of the law, I thought we should all take the opportunity to offer him our alibis."

Faith volunteered her alibi by mapping out her schedule for the morning of the picnic. The day had started with a chat with her neighbor when she'd dropped off her dogs. "She'll happily corroborate this." Shortly afterwards, she'd driven to town, stopping at Joyce's to grab a coffee."

"Yes, I can vouch for her," Joyce said. "And in turn, she can vouch for me."

"Then I went straight to the Gazette," Faith continued. "Mitch saw me going in at nine o'clock. My online activity until Abby turned up to collect me covers the rest of the time. And, no, I didn't have any reason to want to kill Miranda. If, indeed, she was killed."

They all turned to Abby.

"What? I'm still new in town. Why would I want to harm her?"

"Because you're secretly a cold-blooded murderer," Joyce said. "After you witnessed the altercation between Kitty and Miranda, you decided to take advantage of the opportunity." She turned to Joshua. "Are you sure her background check cleared?"

He grinned. "Yes. It did."

Joyce shrugged. "There's always a first time. Maybe you should run a psychological profile and see if she'd be capable of killing someone without motive."

"About that altercation you mentioned," Joshua said.

Abby realized he might not have heard all the details. "For once, I feel I have the upper hand." She filled him in. "So, you see, Kitty might have been pushed too far." Abby leaned forward. "Give and take."

Joshua checked his watch.

"Oh, no, you don't."

"What? I was only thinking it's close to dinner time."

"We'll order room service." Abby got the menu from the kitchen and handed it to him.

"Okay. I do have some information you weren't aware of."

They all leaned forward.

"After you all left the picnic grounds, William Matthews arrived."

"Is he coming back?" Faith asked.

Just as Joshua had been about to tell them about William Matthews, his cell phone had rung and he'd stepped out to take the call.

Abby unclenched her jaw. "If he doesn't, I'll use whatever influence I have with Joyce to get him banned from the café."

They all stood staring at the collage they'd put together to recreate the day of the picnic.

Abby tilted her head. "I don't remember seeing William Matthews and I don't believe Miranda went to the picnic alone. Where is he?" Or, rather, where had he been?

Faith nudged her. "You're the only one who's seen this William Matthews character. He has to be in one of these photos."

"This is interesting." Abby pointed to a photo. "This is one of the first photos I took when we arrived." And Kitty appeared to be coming from the path that led to the secluded area where they'd found the rowboat, she thought.

Faith shook her head. "I think we've exhausted the possibility of her being involved. Her motive would be too obvious. The police would have her in handcuffs by now. Maybe we have to accept the fact a renegade bee really is responsible."

Abby gave a pensive shake of her head. "The more I think about it, the more convinced I am someone had a hand in Miranda's death." Abby's cell phone rang. Checking the caller ID, she growled softly. "I cannot believe this. " She huffed out a breath and answered. "Detective. Either you had an emergency to attend to or you're calling me from a safe distance. Which is it?"

CHAPTER 8

"Come on, Doyle. You can't grumble because I dragged you away from your comfortable bed. You would have grumbled if I'd left you behind." Abby dove back inside the car and drew out a coat. As she sipped her coffee, she watched Doyle take a tentative step onto the still dewy grass. He wagged his tail and launched into a sprint right up to the lake and then back toward her. "That's the spirit."

Abby checked her watch. Joshua had promised to meet her at the lake at eight o'clock. Still no sign of him. Doyle wandered off. Finding a patch of dry grass, he rolled around in it. When he finished, he sprinted toward her, his tail wagging, his tongue lolling.

"How about sniffing out a clue?"

Doyle stood still. After a couple of seconds, he put his nose to the ground and trawled the area.

"Wow. I didn't expect that."

When Joshua finally arrived, he found Abby and

Doyle standing by the trees and bushes overhanging the lake.

Seeing him carrying a couple of coffees, Abby said, "I see you bring a peace offering."

"You can thank Joyce for this. When I went in for my morning coffee, she subjected me to a thorough interrogation." He shrugged. "Joyce has her ways and she managed to get me to admit I was on my way to meet you."

"I'm guessing she threatened to bar you from the café if you didn't bring me a coffee."

Joshua smiled and as he took a sip of his coffee said, "Yes. In my defense, I hadn't had my first coffee, so I wasn't thinking straight. I would have remembered you."

"Okay, drink up. You have some rowing to do."

His eyebrows rose slightly. "What's the plan?"

"I want you to row us to the middle of the lake and then I want to see what happens. I'm sure the boat I saw out on the middle of the lake was the one Miranda was on. Every time I saw it, it appeared to be closer to the shore. It's a theory and I want to test it."

"And you can only do that if I row."

"Would you like for word to spread? I could let everyone know you refused to row."

"What is it with you and Joyce firing from the hip?"

"What can I say? We're women of action."

He grinned. "Women of action who just don't happen to row."

They strode over to the jetty. Joshua got on one of

the boats and gave Abby a hand. Doyle looked at them from the jetty, his little face scrunched up.

"I don't think he's okay with this," Abby said and reached up to grab him. Doyle settled down between her feet. When the boat began moving, he curled up into a tight ball. "I think this is his version of burying his head in the sand."

"Yeah, where's the trust." Joshua laughed. It took them a few minutes to reach the middle of the lake. "Now what?"

"Now we let the boat drift." Abby looked over her shoulder. "Although… Another theory is taking shape in my mind." She gazed over at the other side of the lake. "Is that a jetty I see?"

"Yes. There are several of them. They're all private."

"Have we been assuming Miranda launched her boat from this side of the lake?"

"Yes."

Until now, that seemed logical. Miranda had set up her picnic blanket and basket and then she'd gone out onto the lake.

Doyle took a couple of small steps. Finally, he got up the courage to lean over the edge.

"He's wagging his tail, so I guess he's found his sea legs."

Joshua looked around. "I don't think we're moving."

"Give it some time."

"Even if we move, we'd have to find a mathematician to figure out how long it would take to drift toward shore and he'd most likely want information about the conditions on the day."

"I did some reading on it last night. Lake currents are the result of complex interactions of forces. Knowing about the conditions on the day wouldn't be enough," Abby agreed. "I'm sure a mathematician would also want to take into account the number of boats on the lake and the weight of each person on the boats... and the speed at which they were rowing." Abby grinned. "That would definitely affect the horizontal pressure."

Joshua's eyebrows drew down. "You think it would matter?"

"All those boats moving around? Sure, and even if it didn't, I think the brainy mathematician would say it did just to make the equation sound complicated."

Joshua looked at the water and shook his head. "We probably moved half an inch."

"Do you think it would help if we lean forward? Miranda had been slumped forward. Maybe that set the boat into motion." Here goes nothing, she thought and let herself flop over. Abby peered up. "Well?"

"Yeah, we moved slightly." He checked his watch. "At this rate, we have to assume Miranda launched her boat quite early."

An hour later...

They were definitely drifting toward the shore.

He checked his watch. "I think we need to help this along."

"That's as bad as contaminating the evidence."

"Yeah, and I have a job to get to."

Abby sighed. "I just remembered the oars were missing. Did I already mention that to you?"

Joshua stopped rowing. "The lake is too murky to go searching for them. Actually, I'd have to get a team of divers in from the city and that requires some serious justification."

"I think you're about to get your justification." They were definitely drifting toward the little cove. She held up a finger.

"What sort of measurement is that?"

"I don't really know. Artists do it. I assume they measure angles and distance." She grinned. "If we keep going as we are, we'll eventually reach the little cove."

They lost track of time, but their patience was rewarded when the boat bumped against a thick branch jutting out from the shore and stopped moving.

Abby smiled. "Well, that proves something. I'm just not sure what. My mind is quite muddled."

Joshua looked around him. "Today's wind might have helped speed the process along. I don't remember it being this windy on the day of the picnic."

No, it hadn't been.

"You said you saw the boat out in the middle of the lake. We could possibly assume Miranda was on it and already dead."

Yes, and now they had to figure out how she got on the boat and if she got on it alone.

"Now what?" Joshua asked.

"Now you finish telling me about William

Matthews." Something in the way he narrowed his eyes and looked away told her he was about to choose his words with care.

"He said they arrived together, set up the picnic and then Miranda sent him back home to fetch a shawl for her. He then received a call. According to him, that delayed his return."

So the time it had taken William to run the errand gave him an alibi. "Are you suspicious of him?"

Joshua didn't answer.

"How are his finances?" When he again didn't answer, she added, "I guess you're about to look into them. It would make sense. From what I understand, Miranda purchased a farm and she didn't seem to work."

"Over the years, she inherited a substantial amount of money from various members of her family. Aunts and uncles as well as her parents."

"Did she have any particular ties to the town?"

"Not recent ones. Her great grandfather had been born here but he moved away at a young age."

"You got that from her cousin."

He nodded.

"And who is this cousin?"

"Sahara Johns."

"That's an unusual name."

"She changed it from Sarah. She's studying acting."

So she had something in common with Miranda. "Who stands to inherit Miranda's money?"

"The will hasn't been read yet." Joshua began rowing back to the jetty.

"Oh, I thought we were going to look around."

"Sorry, I have to get to work, but at least we proved your theory. The boat drifted to shore. Quite possibly. Maybe."

Yes, but... Abby looked over at the other side of the lake. So far, they'd assumed Miranda had set off from the jetty. "I still think someone should have noticed a woman in distress. Even if she couldn't call out, she would have flapped her arms or clutched her throat... or something." Abby bit the edge of her lip. "Hey. If the oars are at the bottom of the lake... in the middle somewhere, that would make it the point of impact."

Joshua's eyebrow hitched up slightly.

"You know, the place where the bee attacked Miranda and she lost control of the oars which slipped off... thereby stranding her."

"Are you about to suggest I release the oars to see if they slip away?" Joshua asked.

Abby smiled. "You don't have to let go of them completely."

Joshua stopped rowing. Sighing, he held onto one oar and released his hold on the other. The moment he did, the oar began slipping off the rowlock, but not all the way. "Satisfied?"

"I guess Miranda's panic might have rocked the boat and... what with the boat drifting... the oar might have eventually slipped off."

Back at the jetty, Joshua helped her off the boat.

"Are you going to get divers in?"

He drew his car keys out and eventually nodded. "I have to get going. If you think of anything else, don't hesitate to call me."

"And leave a message?"

He pushed out a breath and threw his head back.

Abby looked up at the sky. "Did you get an answer? I only ask because you appeared to be asking a question. Something along the lines of 'What have I done to deserve this?'"

"Feel free to call me, Abby. I'll always try to pick up… Unless, of course, I'm otherwise engaged in actual police work." He strode off toward his car only to stop. "That didn't come out right. Good work, Abby."

"Aw shucks, you didn't have to say so, but thank you."

Before getting into his car, he pointed to the crime scene tape and wagged his finger.

Under her breath, Abby said, "Let's wave to the nice detective, Doyle. And once he's out of sight, let's go hunt for the button."

"I'm sorry to do this to you, but we can't track mud inside the pub so it's back to Katherine's for a bath." They'd looked under every rock and hadn't found a single button. In the process, Abby had ruined her boots with mud and Doyle…

"You remind me of the way you looked when I first

found you by the side of the road." Abby looked up and smiled. "Hi."

Katherine's eyebrow's shot up. "What happened to Doyle and… you?"

"Oh, I sort of slipped and fell. Can you give Doyle an emergency bath, please?"

"I'm almost tempted to offer two for the price of one." Katherine smiled. "Okay, I have an open slot so he'll be ready in half an hour."

Long enough for Abby to get herself cleaned up and come up with a plan of action. She needed to have a chat with Kitty Belmont.

itty Belmont lived in a cottage only a couple of streets away from the Gazette. She taught drama at the local high school. Wednesdays were her days off and, according to Joyce, she didn't venture out of the house until midday. No one knew what she did with her morning, but everyone knew she then had lunch at either Joyce's café or at the pub. Afterward, she visited a couple of housebound elderly ladies for afternoon tea and a chat.

That gave Abby a couple of windows of opportunity. If Kitty didn't answer her door, Abby would wait for her at the café and then try the pub.

Doyle trotted beside her. "I think you're getting used to regular baths. You look quite happy."

As they neared the house, Abby kept her eyes open for neighbors peering out their windows. "It will be interesting to see what people make of my visit to Kitty's house." Abby knew word would spread in no time. Would they make the connection to Miranda's death?

The moment she knocked on the door, it opened. "Hi... Did I catch you at a bad time?"

"No, I've been expecting you," Kitty said.

Abby couldn't tell from her tone if this was good or bad. "Am I that obvious?"

Kitty gave an impatient shrug. "People around here already know you enjoy asking questions."

"Well, it is my job."

"Come in." Kitty stepped aside and waved her in.

The narrow hallway appeared to run the length of the house with doors on the right leading to various rooms. Kitty waved her in to the sitting room. More spacious than the outside of the house suggested, the room looked like a mini theater with a couch and chairs positioned to face a small stage with a fireplace behind it.

"I hold private acting classes here," Kitty offered.

Abby had never been any good at getting a person's age right. Thankfully, she didn't even have to try. A collection of framed photographs sat on a side table with one picture taking pride of place. Kitty had a wide smile and wore a hat with a large 40 on it. "I suffer from stage fright, so please don't expect me to stand on the stage."

Kitty tilted her head in thought. "Would you like to overcome your condition? I could help you."

Abby had never thought of it as a condition... "I'll get back to you on that one." While Abby sat on the couch with Doyle by her feet, Kitty struck up a pose on the small stage; one hand resting on the mantelpiece, the other on her hip. Dressed in country casual chic that included buff colored jeans and a pretty floral patterned blouse, Abby had no trouble picturing the thespian gracing the cover of a fashion magazine.

"You have questions for me," Kitty said. "The police already interviewed me."

"They did? When?"

"Half an hour ago. Detective Ryan came by."

Joshua hadn't mentioned paying Kitty a visit. Abby cleared her throat. "How do you feel about that?"

Kitty gave a small shrug. "Distraught. I thought Miranda died of natural causes. Now there appears to be reason to suspect foul play. I assume that's the case. The detective was short on information. Anyhow, I can't claim to have been surprised when the police targeted me as a person of interest. Miranda and I never did get along."

Although reluctant to ask the obvious question, Abby still felt compelled to ask it. "Did your personalities clash?"

Lifting her chin slightly, Kitty smiled. "I suppose you could say that. At every opportunity, Miranda practiced the willful intention to take over. From the start, she made it clear she should be the center of attention. She'd studied acting and felt that put her ahead of everyone else."

"When did you last speak with her?"

Kitty studied her for a moment. "You should know. You were there."

"You didn't talk with her on the day of the picnic?" Abby asked.

"No, I had made up my mind to ignore her and enjoy the day."

"And did you?"

"Of course I did." Kitty's voice rose. "Until Miranda had to go and ruin it."

"Did you see her at all that day?"

Kitty appeared to give it some thought, but Abby had the feeling she'd already formulated an answer.

"No, I can't say that I did. Then again, I'd become accustomed to blocking her from my thoughts." She shrugged. "Over time, I learned to ignore her."

And yet, the day Miranda had turned up at the photo shoot, Kitty had sprung into action.

"I guess you knew about her allergy," Abby said.

"No, I didn't. Not specifically. I'd noticed the bracelet with the Red Cross symbol on it, but I'd never had a close enough look to read the inscription."

"And she never mentioned it."

"Why would she?"

To upstage her? Some people thrived on being different... unusual.

Kitty checked her watch.

"I hope I'm not holding you up."

"Oh, no. I was only wondering how long it would take you to ask if I killed Miranda."

"Did she push you too far?"

"Always." Kitty swung away and stared at the fire-place. A few moments later, she turned. "I have a fiery temper. As a child, I'd throw temper tantrums and my poor mother would let me rant and rave until I'd worked it all out of my system. She tried to get me interested in the type of physical activity that would exhaust my energy, but it didn't work. Then the school introduced drama lessons." Kitty stretched her arms upward. "Finally, I'd found an outlet. From one day to the next, I'd become a sweet child with only one purpose in life. I spent my days reading plays and learning lines. The stage became a balm for my soul. It tamed me and then Miranda came along."

Abby shifted to the edge of her seat. "Yes?"

"She ruined everything." Kitty raked her fingers through her hair. "She had a way of unsettling me. Even if she didn't do or say anything, her presence was always enough to throw me off kilter. She could be standing across a room, not even making eye contact, and I'd sense her thoughts."

Abby sat back. "Everything you're telling me points to motive."

"That's what the detective said."

"How did you lose your button?"

Kitty's cheeks colored.

"I saw you fidgeting with your skirt."

Kitty looked away. "The skirt was tight around me and the button was already loose. I'm not surprised I lost it."

"Did you search for it?"

"Yes, of course. I borrowed the skirt from the wardrobe department and I felt guilty returning it with a button missing. Are you suggesting it might implicate me?"

"I wouldn't worry about it. Who knows? A kid might have picked it up."

Kitty strode to the center of the stage and crossed her arms. "Did someone kill Miranda Hoppers?"

"What do you think? Did we just witness the best performance ever? I'm sure I saw the edge of Kitty's lip kick up." At least now she knew Joshua had stepped up his investigation. Who would he interview next? He'd already had a chat with Miranda's husband and cousin. "So who could be next on his person of interest list?" she asked as she strode into the Gazette.

Faith looked up and shook her head. "Have you picked up a new habit of talking to yourself in public?"

"People don't seem to notice." Abby picked up the mail.

Faith laughed. "Wait until you're older with gray hair and stooped shoulders. They'll notice then and call your behavior odd."

"By then it won't matter because I'll be too senile to care." Abby set down the mail and looked up. "Actually, now that I sort of think about it, I've always looked up to my elders, but there were a few I tended to steer clear of. Mrs. Hattie comes to mind. She was a neighbor who lived across the street from us. She'd invite people over for afternoon tea and then refuse to let them in. People were too polite to turn her down, so every week we'd see them trudging up to her front door. Some brought cake and cookies and left them on the front porch. And now that I really think about it, maybe Mrs. Hattie just wanted to get free cake and cookies."

Faith frowned at her. "What is your point?"

"I'm not sure. Maybe I'm trying to say that whatever I do, I'll end up old and gray haired with an abundant supply of cookies. So it doesn't really matter." Abby frowned at the mail. "Do you always get so much mail?"

"Oh!" Faith jumped to her feet and rounded her desk. "I nearly forgot. You've got mail." She handed Abby a stack of envelopes. "I went ahead and opened them."

Abby picked one up and read, "Dear Abby?"

"Yes. I can understand getting one, but there are at least a dozen all addressed to Dear Abby."

"How? Why?"

"Who knows? But I think we can work that into the next issue. You could do a Dear Abby column."

"Why?"

"Because there's an obvious demand for it. I think it has to do with you solving Dermot's death. People see you as the go to person. You know, like the Godfather. What should I take on vacation? Leave the gun, take the cannoli. What day of the week is it? Monday, Tuesday—"

"Yes, yes. I get it, but… Why? Getting it right one

time isn't enough to establish me as the new oracle in town."

"There's an idea. Instead of a Dear Abby column, you could do 'Ask the Oracle.' Everyone could come to you for all their problems and you could solve them."

Abby sunk down on her chair. "And why would I do that?"

"Think of it as doing a community service. This isn't the city where people have access to a large network. There are people living out in isolated farms who don't have the time of day to get out and mingle because they're up before the sun comes up milking cows."

"Joyce would be good at something like this. What would I know about giving advice? Actually, are they all asking for advice?"

"Yes. More or less."

She read one. It prompted her to read another. Looking up, she saw Faith nodding. "Am I reading them right?"

"Yes. Everyone is expressing their concern about Miranda's death and they want to know what to do about it. People are losing sleep over this."

The letters were all anonymous, but everyone had attended the picnic and none of them remembered seeing Miranda. They all mentioned people they'd seen sitting around them.

"I could almost figure out who the writer is by using our photos as reference." Abby laughed. "The whole town might decide to launch their own investigation."

She set the letters aside. "We need a police scanner... or a person on the inside. I'd like to know if Joshua has a list of possible suspects."

"You want to get a step ahead of him? What happened to letting the police do their job?"

"I might be able to work a different angle." Abby lifted her shoulder. "Offer a different perspective but Joshua is being uncooperative."

"You mean, more than usual?"

Abby grinned. "Yes. I'd hoped he'd improve with time but look at how he skipped out on us last night." She sat up. "We need to get the ball rolling."

"I thought we already had."

"I mean, we should seriously start digging around for suspects. People who might have a reason to kill Miranda."

"Did you get anywhere with Kitty? She's the only one with a solid motive. Everyone is suspicious of her."

Abby tapped the pile of letters. "I hope this isn't a lynch mob in the making." Abby grinned. "At least they're not coming after me."

"Not yet! Who raised the alarm?"

"What are you implying?"

Faith shrugged. "You seem to have a knack for finding bodies. That can't be a coincidence."

"Two dead bodies don't make a trend."

Faith gave her a slanted eye look. "Of course you'd say that."

"They were unrelated incidents."

"With one common factor linking them. Two, actually. You and the dead bodies."

"Just as well you're on my side." Abby widened her eyes. "Please tell me you're on my side." She looked down at Doyle. "Doyle? Do you have anything to say?"

Doyle got up and scampered toward the front door.

"Quit snickering. He just wants to go out to do his business." She grabbed his harness. "I'm only taking this out of habit and not because I think he's going to run away from me. Oh, and I might swing by the lake…"

Abby stopped at the door. "How long has Kitty been with Gordon?"

"They've been an item for a couple of years. As far as I know, he's proposed but Kitty thinks she's too old and set in her ways for marriage. Personally, I don't get it. He's clearly in love with her."

How far would a person go for the woman they loved?

CHAPTER 10

"*I*f anyone asks, we're lost." Abby slowed down. What had looked like a private road, had in fact been… "A private road for local residents only. Well, I'm assuming they receive visitors." She knew Eddie Faydon had a house on this side of the lake and she often hosted the girls' Friday night get-togethers, so it wouldn't be odd for Abby to be seen pulling into her drive.

"There is one slight problem. I don't actually have the address." Since arriving, she'd attended a couple of film nights but they'd been held at the local inn just outside of town. "Okay, let's get our story straight. I'm looking for Eddie's house but I'm new in town. Yes, I know. That's wearing thin."

She supposed she could call her brother, but would Mitch Faydon give her the address? Yes, right after asking a barrage of questions.

When she reached the end of the driveway Abby

knew she had the wrong address. Joyce had told her Eddie had used an Australian designer who specialized in Cape Cod style houses.

"This is definitely Victorian architecture. I should know. I've described enough of them in my articles. But we can use the same excuse. We're lost and… We're not from around here."

Doyle curled up into a tight ball.

"I could also use the excuse of you needing a toilet break."

She waited a few minutes to see if anyone approached her. This was Eden's lakeside Riviera. Abby knew some people owned these houses as weekenders… With luck on her side, she'd have the place to herself.

When Doyle refused to get out of the car, Abby had to resort to bribery. "It's the cheese flavored one you like," she said and waved a biscuit at him. He gave her a roll of his eyes and hopped off. "Yeah, I know. Cheap trick." Straightening, she looked around her. There weren't any cars parked in the driveway and all the curtains were drawn.

"Looks like no one's home. We really might be in luck, but we'll play it safe and walk around the outer perimeter of the house. It should lead us straight to the lake." She looked down at Doyle who walked beside her with his head hanging down. "What? You think we're wasting our time?"

They rounded the house and saw the lake. "See, a jetty. That's something to get excited about. You're probably wondering about my theory. So am I." Abby sighed. "Basically, it all comes down to no one hearing Miranda scream for help. If I had an allergy to bees and saw one buzzing within a mile of me, I'd scream. Also, forgive me for mentioning it again, but it was my brightest idea, bees are not active at this time of year. Yes, we've considered the possibility of a renegade bee, but what are the chances?"

Doyle yawned.

"Okay, what if someone introduced the bee into the equation deliberately?"

Doyle looked up at her.

"Aha. I see I have your attention now." The house had its own private jetty. "I've no idea what we're looking for, but keep your eyes peeled open for... foot-prints around the jetty... and a dead bee. Don't give me that woeful expression. It's quite possible. You only need to engage your imagination." Abby looked across the lake at the other side and realized they stood at a diagonal angle to the picnic area. "We need to move on to the next property. Perhaps even the one after that." And they could do it by following the shoreline.

Abby kept her eyes on the ground but didn't see any footprints. The next house they came across also looked deserted. Or, at least, currently unoccupied. Which boded well for her, as the less explaining she had to do, the better.

"This has to be Eddie's house." It looked freshly painted, with a series of French doors facing the lake and a garden in the process of being established.

Abby checked to see where they were in relation to

the picnic site. "It looks like we have to keep walking." Each jetty had one or two boats. A few were motorboats, possibly used for water skiing. "If I'm going to run with this new theory of mine, I'll have to embellish it. Let's see… The killer wanted to make it look like an accident but he had to make sure Miranda died so he did the deed on this side of the lake. Then he hauled her into the boat and…" She stared at the lake. "He pushed it off, letting the current do it's business. He might have done this early in the day, giving the boat enough time to reach the middle of the lake. Note to self… did anyone see Miranda arriving?"

They'd found her about four hours after she'd died. Would that have been enough time for the boat to drift to the other side? When Joshua had rowed them to the middle of the lake, it had taken some time for the boat to begin drifting. "Could the killer have used a motorboat to tow the rowboat out? Yes, quite possibly."

Abby thought she heard the sound of tires crunching on gravel, but she kept going. Finally, she reached a spot directly opposite the picnic area. "This could be it."

Doyle sat down and looked up at her.

"What? You think I need to revise my theory? Why would the killer go to such lengths? Okay. Basically, I can't believe someone with an allergy wouldn't have the antidote with her. I like the idea of the deed being done on the other side of the lake, as in… this side, because… because this is all happening as people are arriving at the picnic. If we could get easy access to the residential side of the lake, then anyone else could too. Now to find some evidence."

As they searched, Abby wondered why Miranda would willingly leave the picnic grounds and trek out by herself.

To carry out a clandestine meeting right under everyone's noses? Yes, it could have happened straight after she sent her husband on an errand. The husband she hadn't flaunted. "That's odd. Most women tend to parade their new husbands around. Why would she keep her marriage a secret?" Abby thought she caught sight of something glittering on the ground but when she bent to pick it up she grumbled with disappointment. Nothing but a piece of glass.

"Maybe she received a call from someone on this side. Hey, that's possible. But, she didn't have a car so she decided to row across." Joshua had said he didn't believe Miranda would set out by herself because she just didn't seem to be the type to do her own rowing… Hearing her cell phone ringing, she looked at Doyle. "See, people get calls." Checking the caller ID, she smiled. "Hey, Faith."

"I just received a tip," Faith said.

"You sound excited."

"That's because I am. I should get a promotion. As soon as you left, I contacted someone. Needless to say they work for the police, but I won't name names."

"Of course not."

"Anyhow. There's been a report about a possible break-in at the lake. Have you arrived yet?"

"Yes, I'm at the lake." Abby looked around.

"The residential side?" Faith asked.

"Yes."

"Have you seen anyone suspicious? This could be the tip-off you've been waiting for. The police are on their way over there."

"Are you saying I'm first on the scene?" Abby swirled around. She couldn't see anyone. "Who called it in?"

"One of the neighbors."

Doyle's soft whimper had her swinging around again. "What is it, Doyle? Did you see someone?"

"Put your hands up in the air."

Abby turned and saw a couple of police officers rushing toward her.

"What was that?" Faith asked.

"Oh... Nothing," Abby said, her tone breezy. "I have to go now and I might be late getting back. Could you maybe do some digging around for me, please..."

Abby tried the door again.

Locked.

She banged on it. "You better be looking after my dog, or so help me, I will lodge a complaint. This is police brutality."

"Pipe down in there."

"When do I get to make my phone call? I know my rights." Okay, so they hadn't actually taken her cell phone but she thought she'd ask. "If you're going to hold me, you have to charge me."

Her breath rushed out in frustration. Abby leaned against the locked door. It had been a couple of hours since the police had hauled her away for questioning. Two hours of sitting alone in this interrogation room. She'd happily answer questions, if only someone would ask them.

She'd been protesting her innocence until her throat ached. Worse. They'd separated her from Doyle and given her the most foul tasting coffee she'd ever had the misfortune of tasting. It didn't even smell like coffee.

The doorknob turned behind her and the door was pushed open unceremoniously shoving Abby out of the way.

"Abby Maguire," a familiar voice said.

Abby peered out from behind the door. "You should take care, detective. I could have jumped you from behind."

Joshua tapped a folder against his hand. "What are you doing in here?"

"That's what I'd like to know. Where's Doyle?"

Doyle scampered in and rushed toward her, his tail wagging, his tongue lolling.

Joshua drew out a chair for her. "Take a seat."

"Are you kidding me? You're going to question me?"

"You don't want to talk to me?"

Now he wanted to talk to her? "You're so hard to read." She sunk into the chair and crossed her arms.

He opened the folder and scanned the contents of a page, his eyebrows drawn down as he read.

"I believe I've been wrongfully imprisoned," Abby complained.

"Sorry. The police officers who apprehended you hadn't heard about you yet."

"What's that supposed to mean?" Abby sounded suitably offended but she had to fight back a gurgle of laughter.

He smiled and gave an easy shrug. "That you're harmless and they didn't know it."

Abby tucked her hair back and lifted her chin. "Oh. I see. So why am I still here?"

He gestured to the door. 'You're free to go, but don't you want to hear my news first?"

Abby leaned forward. "I'm all ears."

"I had a couple of divers search the lake."

Her voice hitched. "While I was in here?"

He gave a small nod. "You were right. They found the oars in the middle of the lake. That only tells us where Miranda Hoppers presumably lost control of the boat."

And the rest remained a mystery. How did she get there? Why did she row out by herself? How did a bee find her? Abby sat back. "I've been thinking..." Not sure she wanted to share her theories just yet, she hesitated.

"By the way, what were you doing on the other side of the lake?" Joshua asked.

"I got lost."

Joshua laughed under his breath.

"Did you know bee venom can be extracted without killing the bee?" She waved her cell phone. "I did some research while waiting to be freed. *Apitoxin* is used in cosmetics."

He gave her a what-will-they-come-up-with-next roll of his eyes. "Why am I not surprised?"

"The *apitoxin* is a long shot and I'm still playing around with possibilities." Another thought struck. Abby sat up. "What if the killer simply got on the boat with Miranda, introduced her to a bee, don't ask me how, and then simply slipped into the lake, swimming away and leaving the boat to drift."

"I like that, but it'll be hard to prove without a witness. Then we'd still have to find someone with a motive."

Abby raked her fingers through her hair. At some point, they had to stop going around in circles. The culprit needed to make a mistake. "Anyhow, back to the bee venom. I wonder how Miranda would have reacted to using skin moisturizer enhanced with bee venom. I suspect she would have suffered the same allergic reaction."

Joshua made a note. "We'll have to run some more tests."

"Really? You don't actually think it's the most ludicrous idea you've ever heard?"

He shook his head. "Anything else?"

"Yes. Has anyone mentioned seeing Miranda on the day?" Abby asked.

"No, but I haven't spoken with everyone."

Abby told him about the Dear Abby letters she'd received. "It seems people are now suspicious of the bee story and they're all claiming they didn't see Miranda. They're starting to put two and two together and coming up with police cover-up."

The edge of his lip quirked up.

"What?"

"I'm trying to picture you running an advice column."

"And?"

He didn't bother holding back his laughter. "I'm now picturing you discussing your advice with Doyle."

"Faith thinks it's a good idea and I'm considering it."

Joshua gave her a small smile. "It's actually good to see you engaging with the community."

What did that mean? For a moment, she became lost in his dark blue eyes and played around with a few possibilities but then reality gave her a nudge and she remembered she still had fresh wounds to deal with.

"What now?" Abby asked. "Do you want me to sign some sort of release form expunging the police officers from any blame of false imprisonment?"

Joshua tossed his head back and laughed. "We wouldn't want to take the right away from you."

CHAPTER 11

"I think the police recruited Doyle to be their snitch. Since we returned, he's been acting strangely."

"How so?" Faith asked.

"He looks at me from the corner of his eye, the way you do when you don't want to be caught looking at someone." Abby strode over to Faith's desk and lowered her voice. "I think we might need to take precautions around him."

"How exactly do you imagine the police will extricate information from Doyle?"

Abby glanced at him and whispered, "I'm not sure, but the police have a K-9 unit and so they must have ways of communicating with dogs."

Faith shook her head. "Are you trying to avoid talking about what you saw at the lake?"

"I didn't see anything." She'd already told Faith all about the divers and their find. "What's most frustrating is that we're no closer to nailing a solid idea. Joshua and I tossed around a couple of theories but nothing stuck."

"I'm actually curious about the skin moisturizer." Faith turned her computer screen toward Abby. "There are videos showing how they extract the bee venom. It's surreal. I've been wondering how I would go about killing someone who had a bee allergy and I could only think about catching a bee in a jar, removing the lid and then somehow holding the jar against the person. Of course, they'd either have to be out cold or a willing participant and I doubt Miranda agreed to be killed."

They watched the video in silence. When it finished, they both looked at each other.

"Powder." The bee venom was somehow collected as powder. "You'd only need to get her to inhale it." Abby sent Joshua a text message. "I'd like to know how the coroner came to his conclusion. Did he find an actual bee sting stuck in her? Joshua said they'd run further tests but I'm not sure I can trust him to share the information with me."

Half an hour later they had their answer.

Hiding her surprise, Abby read the text message Joshua had sent her. "The coroner took into account the physical signs and the bracelet she wore. He's now running further tests and doing another examination of the body."

"Better him than me. It all sounds too gruesome," Faith said under her breath.

"Yes, I agree." Abby sniffed. "Can you smell that?"

She turned and strode to the door. The enticing aroma of sugar hung in the air.

Faith came to stand beside her and moaned.

"What is it?"

Sighing, Faith shook her head. "Joyce is at it again."

"Please explain. I'm still relatively new in this town and while I've become accustomed to the odd behavior of some of the residents, there's still room for surprise."

Faith closed her eyes and drew in a deep breath. "Yes, she's definitely at it. Come on. It's time for a break. You were bound to find out sooner or later."

They strode over to Joyce's Café like mice led by a Pied Piper. The moment they entered, they both stood still and, closing their eyes, inhaled deeply.

Abby drew in another breath and hummed. "Whatever that is, I want one or two. Make it a dozen."

"You'll be fighting me for it." Faith tugged her along.

They settled down at a table and kept their eyes on Joyce who appeared to be deliberately taking her time to come over. When she finally did, both Abby and Faith had their tongues lolling out.

"What is that divine aroma?" Abby managed to ask.

"Portuguese Custard Tarts. They just came out of the oven so you'll have to wait a bit for them to cool down."

"We'll take them all," Abby declared.

"But you haven't tasted them yet."

Abby and Faith shook their heads. "We don't care. We want them. Why haven't we had them before?"

Joyce smiled. "Because I only recently discovered a great recipe."

Awed, Abby asked, "This is your doing?"

Joyce nodded. "I prepared the first batch. The rest will be up to my pastry chef. He's fresh out of school but he's a quick learner."

Abby studied the menu. "I don't see them listed."

"We're her trial customers," Faith said. "If we like them then everyone else will like them, and she'll include them in the menu."

"Okay." Abby sat up. "Let's make this happen. We'll start with coffee because I get the feeling nothing else will suffice."

As they waited for their coffee, Faith asked, "Did they take your fingerprints?"

"No. I'm sure it was all a prank. Do I look like someone who'd break into a house? I'd like to know who called it in."

"Are you talking about the break-in at the lake?" Joyce asked as she set their coffees down and joined them.

Abby nodded. "I'm guessing a neighbor saw me wandering around. A woman and a dog. What's so suspicious about that?"

"Most of the owners work in the city during the week so anyone seen in the area looks suspicious," Faith explained.

"Here comes Eddie. We can ask her." Joyce drew a chair out and waved to her.

"Hey. Did you all hear?" Eddie asked. "There was a break-in at the lake."

Abby put her hand up and smiled at the redhead. "No break-in. Just me. Do you know who reported it?"

"I can only think of one person. Miss Haverstock," Eddie offered. "She's in her nineties and lives out there alone in that house that looks like a mini Scottish castle. She spends her time gazing out the window." Eddie leaned in and whispered, "I don't like to spread rumors, but I'm told she enjoys roaming the tower at night wearing a gossamer white nightgown and carrying a candle."

"She's an oddity in this part of the world," Joyce offered. "I rather like her. Her name is actually Haverstock-Smith. The family has a tradition of hyphenation both parents' names. She never married and insists on being addressed as Miss."

"Out of curiosity, does she have a first name?" Abby asked.

They all looked at each other and then shook their heads.

"We only know her as Miss Haverstock. She's one of the people on our visiting list." Joyce explained a group of them had organized themselves into paying house calls on some of the elderly residents in the area who no longer went out and about. "We take turns so they don't get bored seeing the same faces every week. Would you be interested in joining?" Joyce asked. "You could pick up some juicy stories from them. While they don't get out and about, they always seem to know more about what's going on than any of us."

Abby tried to remember if she'd seen the house. "Is she the only elderly person living in that area?"

Eddie nodded. "Yes, why do you ask?"

"She might have seen something the day of the picnic. I have this crazy idea floating around my head about the killer doing the deed on that side of the lake." Abby drew out a small notebook and pen and jotted down a few notes.

Faith leaned in and read, "Phone calls. Cousin." She looked up. "What's that about?"

"I'd like to know if Miranda had any calls on that fatal day." Abby shrugged. "I also wouldn't mind knowing more about the cousin."

"Oh, you'll get to meet her," Eddie said. "I was over at the pub earlier when she checked in."

"She's here? Why?"

Eddie took a sip of her coffee. "Who knows? Maybe they're holding the funeral here."

A waitress approached and set a platter on the table. Faith and Abby clapped their hands while Eddie's eyes widened.

"You are a goddess," Eddie said. "I usually have to wait until I go into the city to have these."

"You haven't tasted them yet," Joyce complained.

"I don't need to. I can tell just by looking at them. They're good." Eddie helped herself to a tart and, biting into the flaky pastry, nodded. "Heavenly."

Abby and Faith snapped out of their drooling stupor

and both reached for a tart and promptly bit into them. Neither one spoke for the duration. After they'd each had two, they sat back and sighed with contentment.

Abby wagged a finger at Joyce. "If you don't include these in your menu, I will spread the word and organize a demonstration outside your café, day and night."

Joyce looked at Eddie and laughed. "She calls us odd."

Looking at Faith, Abby said, "I could eat three more. How about you?" Seeing Faith nod, Abby added, "But then we have to go back to work. There's some serious digging to do. Then again, this is a brand new era of roaming technology. We might want to stay close to the source of everything that is good in this life and carry out our research right here." She looked up at Joyce. "You should rename your café Ambrosia. We're like bees to honey—" Abby sat up.

"What?" Faith asked.

Shaking her head, Abby said, "I'm sure it's nothing but a sugar rush…"

CHAPTER 12

"*I*s nothing sacred? I should be allowed to entertain wild ideas," Abby said as they stepped out of the café.

"Even so, you have to share," Faith insisted.

"Fine. I just imagined someone dusting Miranda's dress with pollen. You know, something to attract a bee." Hearing Faith's stifled laughter, Abby got her car keys out. "What did I tell you? I knew it would sound absurd."

"Actually, you might be onto something. Lacing gowns with poison goes back to the reign of Queen Elizabeth the first. Maybe even before that time. Hey, I thought we were going back to the Gazette," Faith said as Abby headed toward her car.

"Slight change of plans. Come on, get in." Abby checked for traffic and then turned into the main street. "I'd like to pay Miss Haverstock a visit. If she's the one who reported seeing me at the lake, then she might have seen something else the other day." The wonderful aroma of Portuguese Custard Tarts hung in the air. "I hope she likes the tarts."

Faith hummed. "I'm going to wake up in the middle of the night craving them. I almost wish Joyce had never made them."

"You don't mean that." Seeing Faith reaching for the box of tarts, Abby put her hand on it. "By the way, how did you get on with that search I asked you to do for me?" Before she'd been arrested, Abby had asked Faith to trawl around for any information she could find on William Matthews. Joyce had mentioned seeing him and Miranda driving by on weekends. Abby assumed no one had seen him around the rest of the time because he worked in the city during the week.

"I found several mentions of the name but only two entries ended up being about him."

"How did you figure that out?" Abby asked.

"I narrowed the search to William Matthews, banker. That actually brought up more results. He's also a patron of the arts and sits on a couple of boards. I'm still researching. I downloaded a couple of annual reports but didn't have time to go through them because we were mesmerized by Portuguese Custard Tarts." Faith shifted in her seat. "Joyce is becoming dangerous. I wouldn't be surprised if she renames the tarts and calls them Whimsical Tarts only available at her pleasure."

"She wouldn't be so evil."

"You haven't lived here long enough to see the dark

side of Joyce Breeland. You should ask Elizabeth Charles. She'll tell you all about it."

"Who's she?"

"You haven't met her?"

"Would I ask who she is if I had?"

"She's Mitch's fiancé. Surely you've seen her around town. She drives a yellow VW."

"Hang on." Abby searched her mind. "Come to think of it, yes. I've seen the VW. What does she look like?"

Faith thought about it for a moment. "She's tall. Slim. Long strawberry blonde hair. When she first arrived, she made quite a splash. She'd been on a no sugar diet for years and suddenly she caved in and had a puff donut at Joyce's. She's probably the only other person to ask for an egg white omelet at Joyce's. You being the other."

"How did you hear about that?"

"You're acquainted with the expression 'What happens in Vegas…' well, what happens at Joyce's doesn't stay at Joyce's. Anyway, where was I? Oh, yes. Sugar. After eating the puff donut, Elizabeth had a sugar rush moment and Joyce decided to take the puff donuts off the menu labeling them too dangerous. So she might do the same to the Portuguese Custard Tarts."

Grumbling, Abby turned off the main road. She knew Miss Haverstock's mini castle stood at the end of the lake. This time, she had a better idea of how far to go. Two stone pillars signaled the turnoff into her property. The imposing iron gates were closed but Abby could see a security intercom.

"I'll announce us," Faith offered. "She knows me. Or, at least, she did the last time we spoke. Sometimes I think she pretends she doesn't know me so she can tell me her life story from the beginning."

After a brief exchange, the gates eased open. "Impressive."

"It's all for show," Faith said. "Anyone can just walk along the lake to her place. I think you'll find Miss Haverstock has airs of superiority. Her father had been a judge and there's serious money in her family. This was her family's weekend retreat and I've heard say their house in the city was in the snootiest suburb and surrounded by high walls. Miss Haverstock grew up in the type of world we only read about. Garden parties, shopping sprees overseas, private yachts."

And here she was, a recluse.

Along the way they encountered a gardener raking up leaves on an otherwise manicured lawn. The house really did resemble a castle with a couple of turrets at either end of the bluestone building, large mullioned windows and a door so large it could have been mistaken for a drawbridge.

Abby leaned forward for a closer look. "I assume she doesn't live here alone."

"Oh, no. She has servants. There are people wealthy enough in the area who employ cooks and cleaners but she's the only one I know of who employs full-time staff."

A tall man wearing coattails greeted them at the door. His imperious look suggested he had studied at the most prestigious butler school in Europe.

"Miss Haverstock will see you in the drawing room. Follow me, please."

Portraits and statues became a blur as the butler's long legged stride had them both hurrying their steps.

Miss Haverstock sat on a high-backed chair carved with an intricate design. Going by the darkness of the wood, Abby guessed the austere looking antique piece belonged to the Jacobean era.

Seeing them, Miss Haverstock lifted her chin. Her clear blue eyes sparkled with excitement. Abby guessed she enjoyed having guests.

Her white hair sat like a crown on a heart shaped face. Her pink lipstick matched the color of her twin set. Abby also saw hints of it on her tweed skirt and jacket.

Miss Haverstock gestured toward a couch plump with cross-stitched cushions. "You're that new reporter I've been hearing about."

Faith introduced her.

"And this must be the stray you picked up. My whippets, Lady and Duchess are out for a walk but I'm sure they'll be delighted to meet your Mr. Doyle."

"It's just Doyle," Abby said.

Miss Haverstock looked up at the butler. "Clifford, we'd like some refreshments, please."

Abby held out the box of tarts. "We brought these for you." Settling back, Abby sent her gaze skating around the spacious sitting room. Large windows faced the lake but Abby decided Miss Haverstock would have to have perfect eyesight to see all the way across. Next, she turned her attention to a portrait hanging over the fireplace.

"My great grandfather," Miss Haverstock said.

A stern looking man dressed in severe black stared down his patrician nose at Abby. Deciding they needed to cut to the chase, Abby asked if she'd heard the news.

"Of course I have. Various versions and none true," Miss Haverstock declared.

Oh, dear.

"I could hear the music wafting from across the lake. I told Clifford to keep an eye on the boats."

Abby shifted to the edge of her seat. "Why? Did you expect trouble?"

Miss Haverstock leaned forward slightly. Or she wavered. Abby couldn't really tell. She looked reed thin and Abby imagined her swaying at the slightest breeze.

"It's the lady of the lake," she murmured.

"Pardon?"

"I saw her. I told Clifford to get a closer look. He humored me, I'm sure."

When Clifford cleared his throat, Abby realized he'd been standing beside her stock-still.

"Ma'am, I can assure you, I did not see the lady of the lake or any other lady swimming in the lake."

Miss Haverstock harrumphed. "You need a keen eye, Clifford. You also need to suspend your disbelief. Something I know you repeatedly refuse to do."

Clifford offered a small deferential bow. "My apologies, ma'am."

"When did you see this lady of the lake?" Abby asked.

"The morning of the picnic, of course." Miss Haverstock signaled to the dainty table beside her chair. "I use these."

A pair of opera glasses!

"I have these scattered around the house. My eyesight isn't as sharp as it used to be."

Yes, but… how helpful could opera glasses be? "And what exactly did you see?"

"A woman emerging from the lake."

"Or maybe a man," Abby thought she heard Clifford murmur under his breath. When she looked at him for confirmation, he averted his gaze, but she noticed one eyebrow curved slightly.

"And what did this woman do?" Abby asked.

"She stood by the shore and waved." Miss Haverstock lifted her hand and gave what looked like a royal wave.

"Did you happen to see if she was waving to anyone in particular?"

Miss Haverstock's eyes widened slightly and her lips parted. "Now that you mention it, no. I'm afraid not. The sight of her held me enthralled. She had long tresses the color of sunshine. She made me think of Botticelli's Venus rising from the sea… albeit with clothes."

Abby slanted her gaze toward Clifford and thought she caught him lifting another eyebrow.

"Do you remember what she wore?"

"Yes, she reminded me of my mother. A light colored blouse and skirt." Miss Haverstock's eyes fluttered. "Maybe it was a dress."

"Would you mind if I try them?" Abby asked and gestured to the opera glasses.

"Help yourself. They are quite powerful."

Abby went to stand by the window and, lifting the opera glasses, she looked at the lake. They really were quite good. She strode over to the next window and this time she looked further, toward the opposite side of the lake.

She was about to turn when she caught sight of a shape moving between trees. She must have gasped because Faith came to stand beside her.

"What?" Faith mouthed.

"Nothing," Abby mouthed back and turned to thank Miss Haverstock for her time.

"Oh, you must come back soon. Lady and Duchess will be so disappointed they missed meeting Mr. Doyle."

"What's the hurry?" Faith asked. "We missed out on having more Portuguese Custard Tarts."

"I do hope Joyce changes the name. It's a bit of a

mouthful. Hold on to Doyle, please." Abby put her foot down and drove them out as fast as she could.

"I hope you realize there are speed cameras in the area."

"Out here? Surely the police wouldn't waste their resources on a road with little traffic." She turned into the main road but didn't slow down.

"Don't say I didn't warn you."

Abby bit the edge of her lip. "I'll risk it. Besides, I'm not really going fast. It just seems like it." She checked her mirrors. "I don't see anyone on the road."

"You're not supposed to. The police are quite cunning and know where to hide."

She eased off the accelerator and leaned forward.

Faith laughed. "You think that'll make the car go faster?"

"There was someone at the lake. I'm willing to bet it was a person of interest. We have to get there before they leave."

"We should call the police," Faith suggested. "It's what a sensible person would do. Right?"

Abby chortled. "We're already here. By the time the police arrive, the suspect might have left."

"So it's a suspect now. Returning to the scene of the crime?"

Abby pointed ahead. "There's a car."

"Oh… Oh, dear."

"What?"

"I recognize the car. It has the comedy and tragedy

masks sticker on the back. It's our Eden Thespians logo. Kitty had it custom made."

"No doubt she came back to look for her missing button." Abby smiled. "Let's go give her a hand." And catch her in the act, she thought.

"This doesn't look good for Kitty," Faith murmured. "Why would she be looking for her button near the cove?"

Doyle trotted a few steps ahead of them. He stopped and turned, almost as if wanting to hear Abby's response.

"Remember I pointed out a photo of Kitty walking away from this general area?"

"You don't really think… No, I don't even want to say it. Kitty lives for her acting and nothing else. She would never resort to an act of violence."

Abby assumed everything Kitty had told her about her childhood behavior had been in confidence so she refrained from mentioning it, mostly because she didn't want to be the one to cast a shadow over her character.

"How did you ever see her from so far away?"

"Those opera glasses were quite potent. Also, she's wearing a yellow top." Abby turned her thoughts to the lady of the lake with hair the color of sunshine. If she'd been wearing cream colored clothing… Could she have been at the picnic?

They'd almost reached the path leading to the little cove when Kitty emerged.

She looked up and gasped in surprise. It took her a

few seconds to compose herself and when she did, she lifted her chin and said, "I can explain."

Abby and Faith exchanged a raised eyebrow look. "What do you think you need to explain?" Abby asked.

Kitty folded her arms. "You're wondering what I'm doing here."

"Yes, I suppose we are, but I think we can take a wild guess and say you've come looking for your button."

"It doesn't make me guilty."

"Probably not, but don't you think it would be too much of a coincidence for you to lose it near the little cove?"

"I know it looks bad but there is a perfectly good explanation."

If Kitty didn't come out with it right then and there, Abby would have no choice but to suspect Kitty of trying to buy time to get the details sorted out in her mind.

Doyle sat in front of Kitty and looked up at her.

"Oh, for heaven's sake. Did you train your dog to do that?"

"As a matter of fact, no. Doyle came to me fully equipped with a full range of mannerisms. Which makes me wonder about his previous owner. But that's all beside the point. You were about to explain yourself."

"The day of the picnic I went for a stroll. There's no crime in that."

Doyle tilted his little head.

"Okay, it was more of a blowing off steam walk."

Kitty drew in a deep breath. "Gordon proposed to me again."

And that made her… steamy?

"He… He caught me off guard and I was completely unprepared," Kitty continued.

After what Kitty had told her about her personality, it all began to make sense. The theater gave her clarity and direction. Everything she had to do and say was scripted for her.

"I was afraid I'd say something to put him off for good so I… I stormed off. Not literally. Inside, I could feel myself falling apart, but I think I managed to maintain a calm demeanor. It's only when I got to the secluded path that I started to grind my back teeth." Kitty's hands clenched. "I bent down to pick up a rock." She shrugged. "I guess I needed to vent my anger. Don't get me wrong. I wasn't angry with Gordon but, rather, with myself. I should have accepted his proposal the first time."

Abby could see her eyes softening.

"He's the perfect gentleman. Loving. Considerate. Funny." Kitty laughed. "I've never experienced a boring moment with him. And he cooks." Kitty swung away and growled. Turning back to face them, she said, "I think I lost the button when I bent down."

Abby realized Kitty could not have had anything to do with Miranda's death. She'd already been out in the middle of the lake and had been dead for several hours. "When I arrived I started taking photos straightaway and one shows you emerging from that secluded path. It sort of places you near the scene of the crime but the timing is wrong so I guess that puts you in the clear." Could she say the same about Gordon? She'd wondered about him before but he simply didn't strike her as a killer. His first reaction to Kitty and Miranda's altercation had been to ensure the situation didn't escalate. Also, a couple of the Dear Abby correspondents had mentioned seeing him sitting near them...

Miranda had been killed well before anyone else had arrived. Abby's mouth gaped open and then clammed up in frustration. Miss Haverstock had said she'd heard music and had then seen the lady of the lake.

"What?" Faith asked.

"I have too many thoughts bumping around my head. I think I'm about to explode." Miss Haverstock must have been confused. Miranda had died well before anyone had started playing music.

Kitty's voice hitched. "What if the police find my button?"

"I wouldn't worry about it. We've all searched for it now and no one's found it. For all we know, someone picked it up. Maybe one of the kids. Or we might have trampled on it. It's a bit muddy around there." She refrained from mentioning falling on her butt the day before.

"I wish the police would just catch the killer. How hard can it be? We can't walk around suspecting everyone."

hey drove back to town in silence. Abby would have bet anything Faith's thoughts were spinning around while hers... Well, they too spun, but with a slight difference. She had a wheel of fortune in her head. "Where it stops nobody knows..."

"What was that?" Faith asked.

Abby made a turn and parked the car outside the pub. "It's too late to go back to work."

"You're right. I think we should go sit in front of your crime board and mull this over. I should warn you. I might scream. I never realized how frustrating this could be. How on earth does Joshua do it?"

"It's a pity Gordon Fisher is so nice. He had the perfect motive. I think his love for Kitty would have driven him to commit a crime for her."

Mitch stood behind the bar chatting to a group of customers. Seeing them, he gave the counter a brisk wipe and beckoned them over.

He grinned and said in a singsong tone, "I know something you don't."

Abby grinned right back at him. "Miranda's cousin checked in today." Smacking her hand over her forehead, she then drew her cell phone out. "I just remembered something." She keyed in a message and hit send. "Joshua needs to go through Miranda's cosmetics. What if instead of looking at people who were at the picnic, we should be working our way backward and trying to find proof of a premeditated act. We know the poison can be extracted as a powder and that could easily be mixed in with a moisturizer."

"Look at her." Mitch leaned against the counter. "As giddy as a kid at Christmas time."

"I'd hate to rain on your parade." Faith went around the counter and helped herself to a packet of peanuts. "I'm guessing Miranda suffered from a severe allergy, the sort that crops up in an instant, and any contact with bee venom would have manifested quickly. If she'd applied moisturizer laced with poison at home, she would have dropped dead before she reached the front door."

Abby nodded. "I agree, but Joshua seems more amenable to accepting my ideas. I'd like to think he'll be happy to check this out. I need to have this crossed off the list so it doesn't plague me."

A hand clamped around her shoulder. She didn't need to turn around to know Joshua stood behind her. "I'll go quietly, officer. No need to handcuff me."

"But that's half the fun," Joshua said.

"Did you get my message?" Abby asked.

Nodding, he took the barstool next to hers and ordered a beer. "Are you girls eating or drinking?"

"Abby's decided to dine like a pauper but I'm having a big platter of something," Faith said. "I haven't decided what yet but it'll probably go with a beer so, if you're buying, I'm drinking."

Joshua turned to Abby. "Dining like a pauper? Are you on a diet?" His eyes widened in surprise.

"No… I'm merely trying to eat sensibly, but I could postpone it until tomorrow. It's all about proportions and moderation. Right?"

Faith took a sip of her beer and smiled. "After the number of tarts you indulged in today, you should stick to salad."

Mitch winked at her. "Hannah can whip you up a filling salad. I'm thinking something along the lines of chickpeas."

Abby sunk into her seat. "After all the running around I did today, I think… I'll have a burger. In fact, I deserve a burger."

Mitch nodded. "One Falafel coming right up."

"I said a burger."

Mitch gave her a thumbs up and took the order to the kitchen.

"I can't think on an empty stomach." Abby helped herself to a peanut and turned to Joshua. "Why do you think Miranda's cousin chose to stay at the pub instead of at the house?"

"Your guess is as good as mine. She's here to sort

out her cousin's belongings. Maybe she's afraid of ghosts."

Faith and Abby looked at Joshua, their eyes wide.

He smiled. "What?"

Abby poked him with her finger. "Are you Joshua's doppelgänger? I can't believe you willingly shared that information with us."

"It's the end of a long day for me," he said. "I let my guard down."

"I find that hard to believe." Abby decided he wanted something from her and had deliberately tried to lower her defenses by sharing information. "Why would someone who claims she didn't have a great relationship with Miranda offer to go through her belongings?" Where had that come from? She'd heard it from someone... "Wait, don't answer. William Matthews asked Sahara Johns to go through Miranda's things as a special favor because he either doesn't have the time or he doesn't have the heart to dispose of Miranda's personal effects. Yes, that would be my guess, and we know Miranda didn't have much family. I guess he doesn't either." So the only person he could turn to had been Sahara Johns. Abby wondered how Sahara felt about being assigned the task.

Mitch approached and set a plate down in front of Faith. The large burger had a generous serving of golden fries. He set another burger down in front of Joshua. Abby rubbed her hands. She couldn't wait to sink her teeth into...

"What's this?"

Mitch rounded the bar and got busy pouring a beer. "It's good for you. Eat up."

"That doesn't actually answer my question."

"Think of it as a burger without the bun."

"And the meat." She looked at it. "This isn't meat. It's shaped like a mini burger but it isn't a burger. I thought you liked me. Why would you deny me a burger? Now I have to sit here and watch these two scoff down their delicious burgers."

Without asking, Joshua gave her his burger and took her plate of falafel.

"Did you do that to shut me up?"

"You were sounding a bit whiny," Faith said around a mouthful of burger.

"I actually like falafel and this is the only place around here that serves it." Joshua nudged her. "Also, Faith's right. You sounded miserable."

Mitch shook his head. "She suckered you into it. There's no coming back from that."

Feeling guilty, Abby offered Joshua some fries. "I've been thinking. I don't envy you your job. You have a dead woman and, somehow, you have to trawl around for some sort of proof she was killed. What do you do to switch your mind off death?"

"I catch up on sleep."

"Joshua's being modest." Mitch stepped away from the counter almost as if trying to avoid being within reach of Joshua's ire. "He makes French bread. I've never tasted better. Hannah's been trying to get his recipe for ages."

"You bake?"

"I dabble," Joshua said.

"Heads up," Mitch said and gestured toward the door.

Turning slightly, Abby saw a woman walk in. Her short hair, the color of honey, framed a round face with dimpled cheeks.

Sahara Johns, she presumed.

CHAPTER 14

*M*itch cleared their plates away and smiled at Abby's frown. "Sahara Johns is having dinner in her room."

"Couldn't you entice her to enjoy the comfort, service and company of the bar?"

Mitch laughed. "What do you want me to do? I can't force her to have dinner here just because you want to keep your eye on her."

Abby waved a fry at him. "For once, could you not be so accommodating? How are we supposed to get information out of her if she keeps to herself?"

Faith patted her on the shoulder. "She's in mourning. Give her a break."

Abby turned to Joshua. "How did she react to the news about her cousin's death?"

"The usual way. Shock. Disbelief."

"Did she shed any tears?" Abby knew not everyone reacted to bad news by crying. Emotional releases could kick in as a delayed reaction. If she received news about someone close to her dying, she'd... Actually, she had no idea how she'd react. To date, the deaths in her family had been expected. With most family members enjoying longevity, their deaths had almost been overdue and every funeral she'd attended had been about celebrating the person's life.

"She didn't cry in my presence." Joshua finished his beer. "Do you girls have anything planned for the rest of the night?"

"We were going to sit and stare at Abby's crime board." Faith reached for the desserts menu and scanned the contents. Looking up, she smiled at Abby. "What? I'm not the one making statements about limiting my food intake."

Abby frowned. "I didn't say anything."

"But you were thinking something. Something along the lines of... How could Faith think about dessert after stuffing herself with a massive burger?"

Abby wagged a finger at her. "Earlier you said you ate in moderation. Yet you matched me tart for tart." Abby picked up a menu. "Coffee and lots of it, please Mr. Barkeep." Humming, she tried to guess what Faith would order for dessert so she could get something similar and not feel as though she'd missed out.

Setting her menu down, Faith said, "I'm going to be sensible and have a fruit salad."

"A virgin salad or a groggy one?" Mitch asked.

Frowning, Faith had another look at the menu. "Is that something new?"

"Yes. Hannah's introduced an alcoholic fruit salad. It has all sorts of fruit and orange and lemon juice mixed in with port wine. She calls it the Fruity Rebel. It has quite a kick."

"I'll have to try it."

"Make that two," Abby said.

"Make that three."

Abby looked at Joshua. "I didn't know you were a dessert type of man."

"Not usually, but that sounds too tempting."

Abby rose to her feet. "Okay. Since we've been deprived of Sahara Johns' presence, we might as well retire to my apartment and try to make sense of what we have. Joshua, feel free to join us."

Half an hour later, they were throwing paper airplanes at the wall.

"We should have grabbed a handful of darts from downstairs." Faith tore another page from the notebook and started folding it.

"Everyone is accounted for." Abby pointed at one photo and the next and the next.

Joshua had just caught them up on the latest information about Miranda, which he had kept to himself right throughout their meal.

No bee sting had been found on her body. The over-worked coroner stood by his findings, insisting Miranda had died from a reaction to bee venom. No traces of it had been found in her cosmetics either and, because of his previous lapse, the coroner had been thorough, checking every item in Miranda's possession, including her clothing.

Joshua stretched and yawned.

"What's on your mind, detective?"

"I'm thinking that if I keep this up, I'm going to be out of a job."

"Detective? Are you beating yourself up?"

"I've been in the force long enough to—" He raked his fingers through his hair. "Never mind."

His lagging confidence caught Abby by surprise. Since meeting him when she'd first arrived, Joshua Ryan had come across as being calm, competent, and confident.

"You had a gut feeling. From the start you thought there was something odd about Miranda's death." Abby stood up and checked on Doyle who'd curled up on his doggie bed. He was sound asleep. Although every now and then, his tail wagged. "Anyone else might have closed the case. But you kept at it. Out of curiosity, would you rather be kneading bread right now?"

He chortled. "It does help to clear my head. Also, it puts everything into perspective."

Abby spread her arms out and twirled around on her heels. "What do you do when you hit a wall like this? In your place, I'd chuck it all in and take up knitting."

Joshua laughed. "You hope for a lucky break. You step away and go through all the evidence with fresh eyes. You keep digging."

They'd revisited the scene of the crime several times and Abby had been running through everything they had on a loop until she felt clogged up. "My head needs an enema." She collapsed on the couch only to spring back up. "Hey. Phone calls."

"What about them?" Joshua asked.

"Did Miranda receive any phone calls in the last couple of days before she died?"

"Yes, we've checked them. There were only calls from and to William Matthews. The last one came through early on the day of the picnic. He says he called her to make sure he got the wrap she wanted. Apparently there were two and Miranda could be fussy."

"How's he holding up?" Abby supposed it all depended on the type of relationship he'd had with Miranda. People married for different reasons. Some people allowed their hearts to rule, while others were strict disciples of their reasoning mind. Abby had an aunt and a couple of friends who'd married for practical reasons...

"Well enough. He's been able to answer all our questions."

"Did he seem at all stressed by the experience?" Abby asked.

"He wanted to be helpful. That's what he told us. He spoke clearly and concisely."

"Is that normal?" Abby wondered out loud.

"No, not really. Most victims' relatives have the same attitude. They want to be helpful but they succumb to emotions. That tends to blur their thinking."

William Matthews worked in a bank. Abby guessed that would require a certain amount of level headedness. Abby crossed her legs and nudged him. "How did he react to the news about the bee sting?"

"He didn't believe it at first." Joshua sat up and looked down at Abby.

"Did he know about Miranda's allergy?"

Joshua nodded. "What are you trying to get at?"

"I won't know until the will is read. I assume he'll be the beneficiary."

Joshua scooped up a spoonful of fruit salad juice. "Unless there are special provisions made."

"I guess we'll have to wait and see how Miranda felt about her cousin." Abby checked the time. "Anyone interested in a nightcap?"

"Three Irish Coffees." After serving their coffees, Mitch drew out a chair and joined them. "People are starting to get restless."

"Could you define that, please?" Abby asked.

"I've been hearing complaints all day about the lack of progress." He looked at Joshua. "You need to have someone in handcuffs soon."

"Are you volunteering?" Joshua asked.

"Is this a closed session or can anyone join?" Charles Granger didn't wait for an invitation. He set his glass down and, helping himself to a chair from a nearby table, he sat next to Faith. "I don't normally trek into town during the week, but I was hoping to get some news." He looked around the table. "So… Any news?"

"Faith and I went to visit Miss Haverstock today and she told us about the lady of the lake," Abby offered.

They all waited for her to reveal more.

"That's it. She saw a woman coming out of the lake."

Mitch brushed his hand across his chin. "Miss Haverstock is in her nineties."

"And yet she's been winning her category every year since I arrived," Charles said.

Abby's eyebrows rose. "Category? In what?"

"Archery. I've been holding an annual competition for the past few years to raise money for the hospital. It's coming up in a couple of months."

Mitch laughed. "Miss Haverstock wins because the few people entering do it for the fun of it and not because they've had private tuition."

Charles lifted his glass to his lips only to stop. "Regardless, she wins because she hits the target. Proof her eyesight can be trusted."

"Are you saying we should take her observations seriously?" Abby tried to remember if she'd seen anyone at the picnic with hair the color of sunshine. "Her butler appeared to disagree with what she says she saw."

"I've heard say he has to read fairytales to her whippets every night," Charles mused.

"Are you suggesting he's a disgruntled employee?"

"Sometimes, familiarity breeds contempt. My father

had a butler who constantly told him off. He didn't dare fire him because, privately at least, he agreed with him."

"Let's hope nothing ever happens to Miss Haverstock. If it does, we'll know to point the finger at the butler." Finishing her coffee, Abby thought most women at the picnic had worn hats. She'd seen a few blondes in town, but no one with yellow blonde hair. "Who in town has hair the color of sunshine?"

Joshua cleared his throat. "What exactly did she say about this woman coming out of the lake and why am I only hearing about it now?"

Abby mouthed an apology. "It's been that type of day. I'm sure I would have remembered to mention it... eventually." Thinking about it now, she convinced herself there had to be a connection. "She wore cream colored clothes so I'm guessing she must have been at the picnic." Why had she emerged on the opposite side of the lake?

"Did Miss Haverstock see the woman going into one of the houses?" Joshua asked.

"Oh... I didn't ask. Faith and I were... distracted."

"By what?"

Abby didn't want to mention finding Kitty at the picnic grounds. "I thought I saw someone and I got it into my head it had to be the killer returning to the scene of the crime."

"And?" Joshua prompted her.

"I... I was wrong."

Faith grinned. "Abby doesn't want to say but she thinks she saw a kangaroo."

"From across the lake." Joshua's gaze bounced between them.

Abby nodded. "Miss Haverstock has some powerful opera glasses. By the way, who made the call to the police about an intruder at the lake? Eddie thinks it was Miss Haverstock."

Joshua held her gaze as if trying to figure out the truth about the kangaroo. "The butler, at Miss Haverstock's request. He actually made a point of saying so."

"The man needs to rethink his loyalty." Abby had been a fair distance away from Miss Haverstock's mini castle. Yet the elderly woman had seen her. "We have to find the blonde woman." Or man... Why had the butler insinuated the possibility it had been a man?

Joshua nudged her.

"What?"

He lowered his head and whispered, "William Matthews just strode in."

One by one, they all took turns to look.

"I need a drink and the service here is slow." She strode over to the bar and edged as closer as she could to William Matthews without attracting attention.

She remembered his sun-bleached hair from the day she'd seen him at the photo shoot. Up close, she realized it all came out of a bottle and not the cheap variety. Abby guessed his personal grooming ranked high on his list of priorities.

Without actually feeling his sweater, she knew the label would read 'Cashmere'. If money had a particular scent, Abby thought, so did expensive fabrics. She gazed down at his shoes and decided they were bespoke. William Matthews probably flew to London once a year to be fitted with proper footwear that would be lovingly hand stitched and take six months to make.

A gentle scent hovered around her nose and gradually revealed layer upon layer of a complex fragrance that, again, would have been designed for one particular customer.

Could his job pay for his expensive habits?

Ignoring Mitch's raised eyebrow, she ordered her drink. Back at the table, she was about to relay her observations but everyone's attentions were pinned on the bar.

Turning around, Abby saw Sahara Johns headed for the opposite end of the bar.

"Did she just walk right by William Matthews?"

They all nodded.

"I guess that means they're not on speaking terms."

CHAPTER 15

*a*bby wiped her cheek. "Doyle. Please stop pressing your wet nose against my cheek. If you want to wake me, try barking. And how did you get on my bed?"

Doyle buried his little head under the pillow.

Looking out the window, Abby yelped. "I slept in?" The sun had already come up. "Nine o'clock?" She flung the bedcovers off and leaped out of bed. Doyle rushed after her. "What's the hurry?" Abby pulled out a t-shirt and pair of jeans. "I want to… accidentally bump into Sahara Johns. She's probably already had breakfast. Here's hoping she's a two cup of coffee type of person." A few minutes later, she came out of the shower and raked her fingers through her hair. "Okay, I'm willing to go with the windswept look today. No time to waste."

Abby rushed to the door and looked back to see Doyle circling his food dish.

"Oh, I'm a bad mother. Sorry." She organized some

food and stood back murmuring, "Could you please, for once, scoff it down." She slumped down on the couch. "Okay. Sorry. Take your time."

When she saw him licking the bowl, Abby surged to her feet. "Can you eat and run or do doggies have rules about not doing that for five hours after eating?"

Doyle managed to keep up with her. She rushed down to the bar in time to see Sahara Johns stepping out.

"Missed her." She made a beeline for the door when it occurred to check the dining room. It was busier than usual. "Hey, Mitch. What's up with all the customers?"

"Everyone's heard Sahara Johns is here so they've come into town for breakfast. You just missed her. I sent you a text message. What happened to you? Did you sleep in?"

Abby patted her pockets. "I forget my cell phone." She rushed back upstairs. On her way down again, she noticed a door at the end of the hallway standing ajar. Sahara's room. Had she returned?

She scooped Doyle up and nudged the door open slightly. "I know I shouldn't, but who can ignore an open door?" Whimpering, Doyle buried his little head in the crook of her arm. "Hello?" Abby called out.

A head popped around the corner. "Hi. Can I help you?"

Not Sahara… Abby floundered. "Oh…" She introduced herself. "I just saw the door open and thought maybe the occupant hadn't locked it properly."

"That's nice of you but I'm cleaning the room."

Abby had been staying at the pub for a while and she didn't remember ever seeing her. "How long have you been working at the pub?"

"A year."

"I've been here for a few weeks and I haven't seen you around."

"I usually wait until everyone's left to do the rooms. I'm Steph."

Abby looked around Sahara's room. "I hope I haven't ever left my room in this condition." Sahara wasn't exactly a neat freak. There were clothes strewn about the room. A suitcase sat on the floor empty.

"You're actually good. I often wondered if you realize the pub has room service. Most of the time, I only have to wipe down surfaces and plump up your pillows."

"You can thank my mom for that. It's an ingrained habit." Abby's gaze skated around some more. She had no idea what she was looking for. She supposed she'd know when she found it.

Had she become suspicious of Sahara? Abby sighed. "Maybe."

"Sorry, did you say something?"

"Oh… no. I'm… okay. I'll leave you to it." As she strode back down to the bar, she went through what she'd seen. Had there been any light colored clothes?

"Where are you going with this, Abby?" she asked herself. When Doyle squirmed in her arms she set him down. Why would Sahara want her cousin dead? What sort of relationship had they had? Miranda hadn't come across as a pleasant person but that wouldn't be a solid enough reason to kill her.

"Keeping gentleman hours?" Faith asked as Abby strode into the Gazette.

"Sorry, I didn't mean to sleep in. I'm blaming the combination of the groggy fruit salad and Irish coffee." She checked the mail and saw a couple of Dear Abby letters. "These are still coming in?"

"You're going to have to seriously consider running a column."

"The entire newspaper is my column... more or less." Abby leaned forward and looked at Faith's computer screen. "What are you working on?"

"I've been looking at your photos trying to see if I can find Sahara Johns."

"What makes you think she was at the picnic? I only ask because I assume she arrived in town yesterday."

Faith wagged a finger at her. "Abby Maguire. Surely you know better than to assume."

"Okay, I'll admit I've been playing around with a suspicion. I poked around her room and didn't find any light colored clothes." What if... Sahara had something to gain by Miranda's death? "If, and this is a big if, Sahara plotted to kill her cousin, she'd want to make sure she covered her tracks."

"Yes, that goes without saying. I think it's interesting that she's an actress."

They both fell silent and stared at each other, eyes unblinking.

Faith surged to her feet and strode around the office. Her mouth moved, but no words came out.

"Please share your thoughts."

Faith held up a finger. "Give me a minute."

"Hey, that's usually my line."

"Well, it's contagious." Faith stopped. "When we rehearse a new play, I can't help myself… I always play around with the lines and wonder how I would write them. I don't consider myself a writer, but sometimes the lines sound awkward. That's just me. Although, I know there are some in the group who enjoy writing. So maybe we all do it."

Abby nodded. "I wonder if Sahara can write."

"It doesn't matter. She's an actress so she's always hovering in a make-believe state. What if she has the skills to work out a scene from beginning to end?" Faith sat down. "Let's assume she wants her cousin dead. We'll let Joshua worry about motive. What would Sahara do first? Find a way to kill Miranda without making it obvious."

"You think she somehow talked Miranda into joining her in the boat? That would put Sahara at the picnic…"

"I'm thinking she worked out a plot."

They both took a turn around the room. Doyle followed Abby until he realized she wasn't going anywhere.

Abby clapped her hands. "We need to find out if

Sahara stands to inherit and, until we do, there's no point in even considering her as a suspect."

"What if this isn't about money?" Faith asked. "What if this is simply about getting rid of Miranda?"

Abby grabbed Doyle's harness. "First, we need something to power up our thinking. I'm going to get us some coffee."

Joshua always insisted on having a motive. Abby remembered Joyce asking if people could kill without one.

A senseless crime. "No, there would still be something driving the person to commit the crime. A need to kill. An urge. A desire." Abby cringed at the idea of associating desire with killing. In her mind, desires had positive connotations.

Abby glanced over at Doyle. "I know I said I'd go get coffee. So what are we doing driving out of town? I'm following a hunch." Abby tapped the steering wheel. "I'd like to know if Sahara went out to Miranda's house. I have no idea what type of car she drives, but if we see a car parked outside Miranda's place, I think we'll be able to assume it's hers."

And what would she do then? She could be brazen, knock on the door and offer her condolences...

When she reached the farmhouse, she left her SUV by the side of the road and walked up to the house.

Doyle looked up at her and gave her a doggy version of raised eyebrows.

"Don't look at me like that, we both need the exercise." In reality, she didn't want to announce her arrival. If Sahara had come here to clear out Miranda's personal effects, then... Abby wanted to see it with her own eyes.

"Did you just whimper?"

Doyle trudged beside her, his little head moving from side to side.

"I guess I imagined it." The late Victorian farmhouse with its eucalyptus green colored corrugated roof typical of the era sat in the middle of a large acreage surrounded by a lush garden. The car parked in the driveway looked like a rental. An upbeat tune wafted out of the house. "She must be trying to cheer herself up."

Abby gave the doorbell a try but no one answered.

"I don't think she can hear me." She was about to knock when the music stopped and the door opened a crack.

"Yes?"

Abby introduced herself.

"A reporter?"

"Well, yes... but I also represent the town." She took the opportunity to offer her condolences.

Sahara Johns nudged the door open a fraction more, giving Abby a clearer view of her face.

Her eyes appeared to be bloodshot, almost as if she'd been crying. Abby wished she'd spent time honing her reporter's instinct and hunger for a story. She had friends who didn't have any qualms about aiming for the jugular and asking the tough questions.

Abby softened her voice. "This must be a difficult time for you."

Sahara agreed with a small nod.

"Did you know about Miranda's allergy?"

"Of course."

Abby visibly shivered. "We're all thinking we should get tested. How did Miranda find out about her allergy?"

"A bee stung her while she was on a school trip."

"Wow." Wow? You're a reporter, not a teenager. "It must have been a close call."

"She went to a posh school. They had a nurse on hand."

Abby tried to interpret Sahara's tone. She'd definitely picked up on the derision but there had also been a hint of jealousy.

"Were you there?"

Sahara's lips twitched. "Hardly. Her mom married money. Mine didn't." She looked over her shoulder and then back at Abby. "If you don't mind, I'm busy." Before Abby could say anything else, she closed the door.

"At least I'm not walking away empty-handed," Abby murmured.

Sahara had looked upset. Belatedly, she realized she should have asked about William Matthews. It had been odd seeing them sitting at opposite ends of the bar.

"Almost as if they'd been trying to ignore each other."

A sign of bad blood between them?

She turned and headed back to the car only to realize she'd been talking to herself.

Looking around, she saw Doyle disappearing round the side of the house. "Hey, where are you going?" Abby followed him and saw that he'd stopped before reaching the clearing that led to the rear of the house. He looked over his shoulder at her and then back at whatever had caught his attention. "What is it, Doyle?" Silly question, Abby thought. If she wanted to know, she'd have to see for herself. Abby's nose crinkled. She picked up the scent of…

"Something burning." Stooping down to avoid being spotted from one of the windows, she reached Doyle. "Oh…"

She saw a pile of clothes sizzling under the intense heat of a fire.

Had Sahara been busy burning Miranda's possessions? Hadn't she heard of thrift stores? Clearly she didn't care about the environment…

She heard a back door slam and a second later Sahara strode into Abby's line of vision. She had her arms full of books and…

A cream colored skirt.

"The Eden Thespians wardrobe department is not going to be please." Although she doubted anyone would want to wear a dead woman's clothes…

CHAPTER 16

"*Y*our eyebrows are curved down. What's going on?" her mom demanded.

"I'm parking the car, mom. I always slant my eyebrows downward when I park the car."

"It's actually more of a frown," her mom added.

Doyle sniffed the phone screen.

Her mom yelped.

"I think Doyle is telling you to chill out."

"You could at least have found yourself a proper guard dog. Something with more presence. Like a Rottweiler."

Abby patted Doyle. "He does a good job." Today had been the first time he'd wandered off and she still hadn't decided if that had been a good thing or not.

Looking across the street she saw Joshua's car parked outside the Gazette. Abby scooped Doyle up and dashed across the street.

"What's going on? Why are you running?" her mom asked.

When Abby burst into the office Faith surged to her feet, her phone pressed to her ear. "Here she is. You can call off the search." Putting the phone down she rounded her desk. "Where did you go to get the coffee? Hang on. You're not carrying any coffee. Where's the coffee you said you were going to get?"

"Sorry, I forgot. And... what was that about? Who was that on the phone?"

"I sent Joshua looking for you." Faith frowned. "You went to Joyce's and—"

"No. I didn't... I followed a hunch."

"I don't like the sound of this," her mom said. "Abby. Stop pointing the phone at the floor. If you're going to pursue a dangerous lead, you could at least call someone first."

"Your mom's right. Why didn't you let me know? I could be your backup. Actually, I could be Robin to your Batman."

Abby set Doyle down and gave him a scratch on his belly. Satisfied, he scampered off to his doggy bed. "Would everyone please chill out?"

"You sound flustered. Before, I thought it was just your driving voice, but now I'm not so sure. What's happened?" her mom asked.

"Nothing, mom."

"Abby, I know you're investigating a crime—"

"Mom. I'm a reporter trying to cover the news.

Solving the crime is Joshua's job." She turned to Faith. "What's his car doing here?"

"He came to see you."

"Why?"

"He didn't say." Faith wagged a finger at her. "But he wasn't pleased to learn you'd disappeared."

"I did not disappear. Sorry, next time I'll check in with you."

"So where did you go?" Faith asked.

Abby got a bottle of water out of the mini fridge. Had it been a wasted trip? "I took off on a flight of fancy."

Faith grumbled under her breath. "I think we need to set up a protocol. You can't just go off like that, especially when you say you're going to get coffee…"

Abby swung around. "You've seen Sahara Johns. How would you describe her?"

"Medium height. Short cropped hair. Round face. Sorry, I'm not really good at this." Faith slumped against the edge of her desk. "Are we getting coffee or not?"

Abby looked out the window and across the street at the pub. "I need to stay put. Sorry." She didn't want to miss seeing Sahara returning to the pub.

"Have you hatched a plan?" Faith asked. "It sounds like you have."

"I'm not sure." She nibbled on the tip of her thumb and thought out loud, "What did Joshua want? Surely he must have given you a hint."

"He wouldn't say. You can ask him yourself. Here he comes."

Joshua strode in. "There you are."

"Why does everyone sound surprised to see me?"

"You should have seen Faith ten minutes ago. I had to wrench the phone away from her. She wanted to call the police." Joshua pointed at himself. "Never mind me."

"What's wrong with you?" Abby asked. "You sound weird." Not his usual self-contained self. Had they really thought she'd gone missing?

"Let me see his face," her mom said.

Abby pointed her cell phone at Joshua.

"He looks fine to me. Stand next to him, Abby."

"Why?"

"Because, for once, I'd like to see you standing next to a man and not a dog."

Abby cringed and mouthed an apology to Joshua.

Faith cleared her throat. "Can we get back on track, please?" She strode to the door and locked it. "You're not leaving until you tell us where you went."

"I paid Sahara a visit at Miranda's farmhouse. Like I said, I just followed a hunch. When I saw her leave the pub this morning, I assumed she'd be headed there—"

Faith put a hand up. "Stop right there." She dashed off into the back room.

"I didn't know Faith could be so bossy," her mom said.

"Yeah, but we love her."

A moment later, Faith reappeared. "I get the feeling

that whatever you're going to say needs to go on the whiteboard." Faith gave her a director's cue. "Action."

"I spoke with Sahara Johns." Abby tilted her head and looked upward.

"That's Abby's thinking look," her mom said.

"She was burning stuff and now that I think about it, she probably got some smoke in her eyes and that's why they looked bloodshot."

Faith got busy writing it all down. "What else?"

Abby's shoulders went up. "I don't understand why she'd do that."

"To get rid of evidence," Faith suggested.

They all looked at her. Abby even remembered to point the phone in her direction so her mom could look at her too.

"Who's Sahara?" her mom asked.

"It's Miranda's cousin. She's here clearing out her stuff." Abby clicked her fingers. "Last night when she came down to the bar, William was there but she didn't sit with him. Are they even on speaking terms? Can you enlighten us, detective?"

"I've only spoken with them individually," he said.

"Did William Matthews ever mention Sahara?" Abby clicked her fingers. "Of course he did. You said something about him asking Sahara to clean out Miranda's things."

Joshua shook his head. "Actually. You're the one who reached that conclusion."

"Abby tends to fill in the gaps," her mom offered. "Also, she gets impatient when people don't answer straight away. I bet anything she's rolling her eyes now."

Joshua and Faith nodded.

"It's a habit she picked up as a teenager," her mom added.

"Mom, you're about to be disconnected." Abby ended the call. Seconds later, Faith's desktop computer beeped.

Faith grinned and, mouthing an apology, she swiveled the screen around. "Can you see us, Eleanor?"

"Yes, thank you, Faith."

Shaking her head, Abby asked, "Where were we?"

"Trying to determine what sort of relationship Sahara has with William," her mom offered.

"A needs must relationship?" Faith suggested.

Abby crossed her arms and stared at the whiteboard. "Yes, but why would they ignore each other? Doesn't that ring alarm bells?"

"What would people say if they saw them together?" her mom asked.

"They're both supposed to be in mourning," Abby said. "Someone they had a connection with died. There's nothing odd about them being together. I think there's something very suspicious about them—" Going out of their way to pretend they're not on speaking terms, Abby thought.

"Abby, we don't all have the ability to fill in the gaps."

Deep in thought, Abby didn't know if that had been Faith or her mom.

"How about I go get us some coffee?" Faith offered.

"Not for me, thanks." Joshua waved at Abby's mom. "I have to get going."

Abby snapped out of her reverie. "Wait. You didn't say why you came?"

"Oh… the coroner ran more tests and performed a full autopsy and ran further tests."

Abby didn't want to hear about the details. She'd watched enough TV shows to know that involved a lot of cutting up and weighing of inner organs.

"He found bee venom residue in her lungs. Miranda inhaled the bee venom."

"Would knowing this from the start have made a difference in your investigation?" Abby's mom asked.

"Sorry," Abby whispered. "My mom has a thing about thoroughness. The coroner is lucky she's not in a position to hire and fire." She turned to the screen. "Mom, he sort of identified it. Remember, this is a small town. I think it's safe to say we're lucky he even had the time to look into it as quickly as he did."

"He actually came from the city," Joshua explained.

Abby wondered if they might need to get their own medical examiner. She turned back to Joshua. "What's come over you? You've gone out of your way to come here and share that information? Why?"

"I'm wondering that myself," Joshua said. "Please stick to playing around with a crime board. No more chasing after people."

After Joshua left, her mom said, "Abby, you should be nicer to him. The fact he shared information with you means he credits you with some abilities. He thinks you can help out. It's not unusual for police to engage with consultants…"

Inhaled venom.

Could that be proof Miranda had known the killer?

Faith waved. "I'm going to get us some coffee. I should only be gone five minutes. If I'm not back by then, you should contact the café and if they can't help you, please feel free to call the police."

Abby looked out across the street just as a car pulled up outside the pub. Sahara's car. She emerged carrying a handful of books. Before Sahara could disappear into the pub, Abby dove for the camera and snapped a couple of photos.

"What was that?" her mom asked.

Abby strode to Faith's desk and turned the screen to face her.

"What are you doing? I can see you but I can't see what you're doing on the computer."

"I just took a photo of Sahara and I want to print it out." Before she did that, she decided to play around with the image.

"Let's give her longer hair." Doyle stirred and looked at Abby. "Did I wake you? Sorry. Although I shouldn't apologize. I've heard you roaming around the apartment in the middle of the night. If you didn't take so many naps during the day, you'd sleep right through the night."

"Are you enjoying having a pet?" her mom asked.

"I haven't really thought about it."

"I'm sorry you couldn't have a pet growing up." Her mom sniffled. "I dropped in on Mrs. O'Hara next door. She recently had a wisdom tooth pulled out. I swear I didn't stop sneezing the whole time I was visiting. When her husband passed away, she acquired two dogs to keep her company. They're the cutest little creatures but very hairy."

As her mom chatted away, Abby changed the color of Sahara's hair. Her dark eyebrows suggested honey blonde wasn't her natural hair color, so she made it darker.

"I can't see what you're doing but if your expression is anything to go by, you're surprised."

"Yes. I wonder how I'd look as a blonde."

"What's come over you? You've never been unhappy about your looks."

Abby wagged a finger at the screen. "What would you have said if I'd complained?"

"I would have told you to get over yourself and be grateful you have a functioning body. You should focus on the positives and count your blessings."

Let's make her a real blonde, Abby thought. She tried a lighter tone. Hitting the wrong button, she ended up making Sahara's hair white. With a few clicks, she changed it to… "Sunshine blonde."

Abby played around with the image and then printed

a copy and showed her mom.

"Who's that?" her mom asked.

"It's Sahara." Biting the edge of her lip, Abby studied the picture.

"That's your worried look. Something's bothering you."

Abby nodded. "I'm still thinking about William Matthews and Sahara standing at opposite ends of the bar. It felt too obvious. Almost as if they'd both agreed they shouldn't be seen in public together." She sat forward and went through the files on Faith's computer until she found what she wanted. "Can you do me a favor, mom? I'll send you a couple of annual reports. Faith said she'd go through them but it wouldn't hurt if someone else had a look. Can you see if you can find any connection between William Matthews and the theater?" She attached the documents and emailed them to her mom.

Grabbing her keys, she shot to her feet.

"Abby? Where are you going?"

"I'll talk to you later, mom. Come on, Doyle. We're going for a little drive." Looking over her shoulder, she said, "Mom, tell Faith I'll be back shortly."

"What? You can't leave me in charge of the office."

Abby laughed. "You can be our temporary virtual assistant."

"Wait. At least turn the screen around so I can look at the front door. What if someone sneaks up on me?"

"Mom, you're 8,000 miles away. You'll be safe."

"People die of fright. Now do as I asked, please."

CHAPTER 17

"**A**bby Maguire to see Miss Haverstock, please."
She looked down at Doyle and whispered, "I
guess I should have included you. Sorry."

The gates opened silently. Abby took a moment to
appreciate the copse of trees lining the driveway. They
were mostly evergreens. Seeing the tall pines swaying
slightly in the breeze, she thought about the rowboat
drifting toward shore. It had to be a possibility…

"I think you'd love romping around the lawn. I
never stopped to think about it. You probably lived in a
house surrounded by a garden."

Clifford opened the front door before she could ring
the doorbell. "Right this way, please."

This time he showed her through to a conservatory.
The glass structure had an indoor lily pond with a statue
of a cherub in the middle.

Miss Haverstock waved and approached her from the
far end. She strode at a sedate pace, smiling and admiring

the lush display of tropical plants. Out of nowhere, two whippets appeared and dashed toward Doyle. They danced around him and then leaped back and froze into a snapshot pose. Moments later, they resumed dancing around him. Poor Doyle. He looked right out of his element.

Miss Haverstock clapped her hands. "They are delighted with Mr. Doyle. Is he naturally shy?"

"I think he's a little overwhelmed."

"I'm so glad you remembered to bring him back for a visit."

"Actually, there's something I wanted to show you." Abby drew out the photo she'd printed of Sahara.

Miss Haverstock took the photograph and, slipping on a pair of glasses, she studied it. Without saying anything, she strode toward the end of the conservatory and held the photo up.

It took a moment for Abby to realize Miss Haverstock was using the lake as a backdrop.

"This is the lady of the lake."

Doyle hurried past Abby and beat her to the car. "If I didn't know better, I'd say you were relieved to get out of there. I don't know what you have to complain about. You had two beautiful doggies vying for your attention." Admittedly, they had both been overly enthusiastic…

Doyle pawed at the car door.

"Hold your horses."

As soon as she opened it, he scrambled inside and curled up into a tight ball. When they drove past the gates, he looked up as if to make sure it was safe.

"Yeah, you can come out of your shell now."

He wagged his tail and leaned out the window to look back.

As they drove away, Abby called the Gazette to let Faith know she hadn't been kidnapped.

"I've had to drink two coffees," Faith complained. "When I came back I found you'd disappeared again and left your mom to look after the front desk. Mrs. Doggett was walking by when she heard someone calling her. It was your mom. Apparently, she greeted everyone who strode by. She sent a few people running for their lives. They thought computers had finally taken over. Anyway, I found your mom and Mrs. Doggett chatting. They were exchanging recipes. So where did you get to?"

Abby waited a second to make sure Faith had finished her caffeine-induced speech. "I went out to get some empirical evidence." Belatedly, Abby wished she'd mocked up a couple of photos, one with Sahara and the others with some other people. Would Miss Haverstock have picked the one with Sahara?

The fact she had identified her as the lady of the lake really proved nothing. How did one confront a possible suspect without hard evidence?

"I'll talk to you soon." She disconnected the call and

called Joshua. When he actually picked up the call, Abby sounded like a maniac muttering nonsense.

"Did you investigate the bonfire?" she asked. "There might still be a clue."

Joshua sighed. "Where are you going with this?"

"I don't know yet. Anyway, I just thought I'd tell you about the photo."

"Abby. Leave it alone and let the police do their job."

"So you're not going to follow it up?" Before he could answer, she disconnected the call and, instead of turning toward the town, she headed in the opposite direction.

As she approached Miranda's farm, Abby kept an eye out for any cars approaching. She wanted to take a closer look and see if she could find any debris left from the bonfire Sahara had set, something she wouldn't be able to do if Sahara was around.

"We're in luck. There's no one here." Seeing Doyle shrinking back, Abby laughed. "And there are no lady dogs around either. Come on."

Abby prodded the smoldering pile with the tip of her boot. "Ashes to ashes." Even a forensic scientist would need luck to make any sense of the debris. Stooping down, she picked up a stick and poked around. Nothing left.

Determined to find something, she dug around some more, poking at the pile with the stick, first with care and then with stabbing motions. Meanwhile, Doyle sniffed around, got too close and sneezed.

"There should be a law against people burning stuff. It's not good for the environment. I have a good mind to call the police and harass them until they issue a fine."

When her cell phone rang, she ignored it and continued her search. There had to be something. Her phone rang again and she suspected it wouldn't stop until she picked up.

A breath filled with frustration shot out of her and she answered. "Joshua, I'm busy."

"And I'm at the Gazette and you're not," he said.

"What are you doing there again?"

"Making sure you stay out of trouble, but I see I'm already too late and you're sticking your nose where it doesn't belong. Stop what you're doing and come back."

Doyle whimpered.

"Or what?"

"Or I'll go there and arrest you for tampering with police evidence."

"So you admit this could be evidence."

Joshua's throaty grumble made Abby smile.

"There's no law that says a reporter can't go around looking for a story." Abby hung up and growling, she stabbed the pile of ashes. She was about to hurl the stick away when she noticed something sticking to the end. "Well, hello. What's this?" A small clump with a tuft of hair…

She held it up to the light. Most of it was charred beyond recognition but a couple of strands remained, the tips looking light enough to suggest this might have been part of a wig.

Doyle barked.

"Hush. What's come over you? You don't bark."

The distinct sound of a rifle being cocked had Abby swirling around. She'd never heard the sound in real life but she'd watched enough movies to recognize it.

Before Abby's fight or flight response kicked in and clogged up her throat, she managed to say, "Hi."

Sahara Johns didn't answer.

Abby rose to her feet and smiled. "I guess you're wondering what I'm doing here." She took a step only to stop when Sahara nudged the rifle forward.

Abby lifted her hands. "Hey. You should be careful with that. It might be loaded."

"Yes, it is loaded," Sahara said. "I made sure of it."

"Oh." Abby looked around her and saw Doyle looking straight at Sahara, growling through his tightened lips. "Stay, Doyle." She prayed he wouldn't do anything heroic. Something told her Sahara knew how to handle a gun.

"This is what's going to happen," Sahara finally said. "Yes. I am going to shoot you and you're going to drop dead, but I don't want you to go without knowing how the rest will unfold."

Abby had trouble swallowing.

"I'm from the city so I'm not used to living in such an isolated area," Sahara continued, "I thought I heard noises. When I came out to investigate, I saw you. Of course, I recognized you so I lowered my gun but your dog startled me and I jumped back. Then I tripped and that's when the gun went off."

Abby hated to admit it but Sahara had managed to convince her. It could work. It really could.

"Why would you go to all that trouble?" she asked.

Sahara snorted. "Because you're onto something. Either you've figured it out or you're about to."

Abby forced her lips to curve into a smile. "Oh, you give me far too much credit."

The back door swung open and shut. It took all of Abby's efforts to tear her gaze away from the rifle to see who it was even though she already knew.

William Matthews strode toward Sahara. "What are you waiting for?"

"I'm savoring the moment. Do you realize how close she came to ruining it all for us?"

"It was you, out at the lake," Abby said, her voice remarkably steady. "You wore a wig and dressed in cream colored period clothes."

Sahara turned to William. "See? I told you. She's a smart cookie."

Abby held her phone up. "Detective Joshua Ryan heard everything I just said and he's on his way." She wished. Why had she hung up on him?

"Liar. You hung up on him."

"The police are already onto you. They've put everything together. They know you were at the picnic."

Sahara's lips tightened.

"Somehow you convinced Miranda to go out on the lake. When you got to the middle of the lake something happened." Surprised by what she'd said, Abby stopped. Sahara enjoyed having an audience. Just now, she could have shot her dead, but she'd wanted to take center stage. Abby imagined her on the boat thinking about all the people arriving at the picnic. Her audience.

"When you were out in the middle of the lake," Abby continued, "You did exactly what you did just now. You told Miranda you'd come to the picnic to kill her." Again she stopped but only because she needed to run through the events. Once the reality of her dilemma had sunk in, Miranda would have screamed for help. "You had bee venom with you and you blew it in her face. She breathed it in." That would have taken care of her screaming. "And as she struggled for breath, you told her the rest. How you'd conspired to kill her." Abby scooped in a breath. Had Sahara met William before Miranda? Had they plotted to murder her for her money? They were clearly in on this together.

Sahara smiled. "She had everything. The big house in the glitzy suburb. The beach house. The holidays. You name it, she had it."

"So why did she come to live here?"

"Because she knew she'd be able to outshine everyone in a small town."

"Yes, but... why kill her?" Jealousy seemed too petty.

"She could have invested in my play but she refused unless she got to play the leading role."

Abby's mouth gaped open. Yes, she could see it now. "You asked her to invest in your play and when she refused, you tried to raise the money yourself. That's how you met William." Or maybe she'd met William first. He worked in a bank. It would make sense if Sahara had tried to secure a loan. Then again, if she didn't have any money, she wouldn't have any collateral either. "How did you two hook up?"

"I met him at an opening night for a play. He was a guest and I was serving cocktails." Sahara shook her head. "It wasn't fair. I had the talent but I had to work nights serving drinks just to make ends meet. Miranda had more money than she knew what to do with."

Okay. That took care of the motive, but how had Miranda ended up married to William?

"I knew she wouldn't name me in her will. I also knew my cousin inside out. The moment she saw me with William, she had to have him for herself. So I made sure she saw us together."

Wow. Only a devious mind looking to cut corners could work all that out. The average person would get a second job…

"The police are on their way," Abby insisted. "They'll never believe you killed me by accident. I was just on the phone—"

"I know. I heard you. And you're lying. Just like you were lying when you said you hadn't hung up. No one's coming to your rescue."

Abby produced a smug smile. "There's a witness. Someone saw you coming out of the lake. She identified you today." Abby nodded. "I told her about you and how after you blew the bee venom in Miranda's face, you dived into the lake and swam to shore." She looked at William Matthews. "And he was waiting for you on the other side. You probably watched everything unfold. Heck, you probably even waited until the boat drifted to the shore."

Sahara laughed. "Just think. Now you know the truth, you can die in peace. You have to admit, I've been very nice about it."

Abby scoffed. "Your plan is not going to work. Do you think I came here without telling the others what I know? By now, word will have spread to everyone. It's that type of town." Shaking her head, Abby smiled as she thought two could play at the game of plotting. "This is an interesting turn of events."

"What are you talking about?"

"Get it over and done with and shoot her," William said.

Abby laughed. "Yes, Sahara. Shoot. He needs you to shoot so he can finish the job."

"Sorry, time's up." Sahara took aim.

"He's pointing a gun straight at you. The moment you shoot me, he'll shoot you." Abby managed a chuckle. "Why share the money when he can get to keep it all to himself?"

"Don't listen to her, Sahara."

Abby saw her nibbling the edge of her lip. "Of course, he won't get away with it because he doesn't have a solid plan the way you have. I have to admit, the story about you tripping over had me convinced. But how is he going to explain two dead bodies?"

"Shoot her. Shoot her now." William made the mistake of stepping on a twig.

Sahara swung around. In that split second when the gun was pointed away from her, Abby knew she had to act. Without thinking of the consequences, she lunged for her.

Of course, she wouldn't have taken the risk if she hadn't spotted Joshua making his way toward them.

Luckily, he acted quickly, sprinting toward them, his gun drawn and aimed at Sahara.

Moments later, Abby would remember seeing Joshua's expression turning to steel. She'd even spared a thought to how much trouble she'd be in.

When her body connected with Sahara's, they both tumbled to the ground. Snarling, Doyle clamped his mouth on Sahara's hand.

Luck was on her side. William Matthews only thought of himself as he took off and tried to save his own skin.

Even in her moment of defeat, Sahara still tried to snatch back some ground. She somehow got her finger around the trigger and pulled.

*D*etective Joshua Ryan strode into the Gazette, his scowl firmly in place. "You were lucky to walk away with a few bruises. I thought I'd tell you just in case you didn't hear it the last dozen times I said it."

Abby lifted her elbow. "And a scratch. Don't forget the scratch." Picking up her coffee cup, she smiled. "Joyce named a coffee after me. The Abby Maguire. You should try it. It's infused with chocolate that sits at the bottom and gradually melts."

Joshua hitched his hands on his hips. "I'm here to issue an official police reprimand."

"Pull up a chair, detective. Smile and be happy."

The edge of his lip twitched.

"Has William Matthews been apprehended?"

He nodded. "Road block." He stooped down and gave Doyle a scratch behind the ears.

"My little hero." Who couldn't tell right from left,

Abby thought. While he'd clamped onto Sahara's right hand, her left hand had been free to reach the gun and pull the trigger. The gunshot had only made William run faster. He'd been lucky to walk away unscathed.

Savoring her coffee, Abby said, "I could live to be a thousand and still not manage to get my head around the reasons why people kill for money. It goes beyond greed."

"You need to consider sociopathic tendencies," Joshua offered. "They are a must if you're going to kill someone."

Faith came out of the storeroom saying, "The white-board has been put away. I hope that's the last time I have to bring it out." Looking up, she smiled. "Hello, you're back."

"Yes, as promised. I went to Joyce's Café and straight back to the office. Your coffee is getting cold."

Faith smiled at Joshua. "Have you come to tell Abby off again?"

"Don't encourage him."

"Did I hear someone mention sociopaths?" her mom asked.

Abby grumbled under her breath. "Faith, could you give me a heads up before you video chat with my mom?"

"Sorry, I forgot. You'd stepped out to get coffee. We were chatting and she had to go answer the front door and I went to put away the whiteboard." Faith shrugged.

"Yes, mom. Sociopaths." Abby made a winding motion with her finger.

"I think everyone should be tested," her mom said. "Before we're allowed on the road, we have to obtain a license…"

Faith sipped her coffee and moaned. "What is this heavenly concoction?"

Abby grinned. "It's the Abby Maguire. I've had a coffee named after me. I actually feel short-changed. Joyce usually puts more thought into naming her coffees."

"Maybe we could make suggestions. The Abby Maguire Action Packed Shot." Faith lifted her mug in a salute. "The Abby Maguire Scoop."

Giving Doyle a final scratch, Joshua straightened. "Yes, yes. Enough with the accolades. We don't want to encourage her. Abby could have been killed."

Faith wagged a finger at Abby. "You thought working in a small town newspaper would be boring."

Abby tapped her chest. "Be still my heart. Any more excitement, and I'll expire."

Joshua frowned. "I can't tell if you're being sarcastic or not."

"I'd tell you but then that would blow my international woman of mystery cover." Abby finished her coffee. "Joyce must have put some other secret ingredient. I want another one. I'm going back to Joyce's. I think we should all go and celebrate… Again."

"Wait," her mom said, "What about me?"

Faith waved her cell phone. "I've got you, Eleanor."

As they headed to Joyce's her mom said, "Oh, it's so nice to get out of the office."

Joshua nudged her. "I didn't realize you'd acquired a virtual assistant."

"Yes, apparently so. Actually, I can't complain. Mom went through the annual reports Faith had downloaded and she found a photo of William Matthews and Sahara at an opening night. It proves they knew each other. That will come in handy. I'm sure she'll insist they didn't have any contact."

"Sahara is actually pointing the finger of blame at William, saying he's the one who put her up to it and he masterminded the plan."

Abby asked, "Has Sahara pleaded temporary insanity? Most killers tend to do that."

"She can try but I doubt it'll be taken seriously. She went to a lot of trouble to get that bee venom. It can't get more premeditated than that."

Abby tilted her head. "I can almost understand her reasons for killing Miranda, but William Matthews has me baffled. He must be a good actor to have convinced Miranda he loved her."

A cacophony of screams, screeches, yowls and hoots had them all turning around.

"What now?" Abby asked.

Kitty Belmont appeared from around the corner, her arms waving in the air.

"She's finally lost her marbles," Faith said.

"I found it. I found it." Kitty skipped toward them.

"What is she talking about?" Abby asked. "Oh, hang on. Really?"

Kitty held up a button. "I found it. I found it. Detective. I found it. This proves I'm innocent."

"Should we tell her?" Faith asked.

"Hang on. I need some photos first. This is my scoop. Kitty Belmont's lap of victory around the town of Eden, celebrating her innocence."

When Kitty finally calmed down, she explained she'd been cleaning her car when she found her missing button lodged between the seats.

Striding into Joyce's Café, Joshua turned to Abby. "Does she know she was never really a suspect?"

Abby smiled. "Oh… Maybe for a brief moment, she might have been."

"Where did she get the idea she was a suspect?"

Abby shrugged. "Come on. You need to try an Abby Maguire. It's the best coffee Joyce has brewed to date."

Made in the USA
Monee, IL
07 February 2024

53099259R00125